SWORD OF DAMOCLES

With the other scientists in the control room, he gazed upon the blacker-than-black void, with its icy, unwinking stars, the prominence-girdled sun with its incredible corona, and the slowly receding Earth, the stars reaching to the pinkish band created by the atmosphere.

Yet there was an odd look about Earth, and it seemed to lie in the cloud formation—as distinct from the atmospheric envelope. It looked almost as though a faintly relective cloud existed beyond the main cloud covering. A gigantic ring of cloud, going right round the Earth, and having something of the appearance of the rings of Saturn, though much nearer to Earth than the rings of Saturn are to Saturn. It was an inescapable, mystifying phenomenon, which had been created by the atomic war.

Meredith, the weatherman, was the first to comment upon it. His interest in the formation was something more than that: it was an absolute fascination as he gazed through the big outlook port.

"That's got to be studied out carefully," he said, turning. **"I never saw anything like it."**

ABOUT THE AUTHOR

JOHN RUSSELL FEARN began his career as a science fiction writer in 1933, when *Amazing Stories* serialised his first novel *The Intelligence Gigantic*. Over the next decade Fearn sold more than 100 stories of all lengths under his own name and numerous pseudonyms to the leading sf magazines in both America and England. As versatile as he was prolific, he used a variety of styles that ranged from universe-destroying "thought variants" to intensely human stories.

In 1950 Fearn was commissioned by the UK publisher Scion Ltd to write a long series of sf paperbacks under the contractual pen name of "Vargo Statten." They became best-sellers and have been reprinted all over the world in numerous translations.

Earlier, Fearn had created science fiction's first super-heroine, Violet Ray – "The Golden Amazon" – and in 1944 his first "Amazon" novel appeared in England. Reprinted as a "Novel of the Week" in the Canadian magazine *The Star Weekly*, it proved so popular that Fearn was commissioned to write an entire series of open-ended sequels, ending only with his death in 1960. The early "Golden Amazon" novels have been reprinted as hardcover and paperback books on both sides of the Atlantic, and currently New York publishers Gryphon Books have began an ambitious programme of reissuing the entire Golden Amazon series in uniform paperback editions.

During his lifetime (1908-1960) Fearn also published an enormous amount of detective, western, and other types of popular fiction, much of it under pseudonyms which are still being discovered by Fearn's literary executor, Philip Harbottle.

Cosmos Books are proud to present this first-ever book publication of two of Fearn's finest sf stories, representing both his early and later work – *Manton's World* (a short novel) and *Creation's End* (a novelette).

MANTON'S WORLD

by

JOHN RUSSELL FEARN

Cosmos Books

Cover art by Ron Turner.
Frontis by Ron Turner.

Printing History:
Magazine version published in *Toronto Star Weekly*: June 7, 1958
First Book Edition: December 1999

ISBN: 0-9668968-3-1
Library of Congress Catalog Card Number: 99-067452

Cosmos Books are published by Philip Harbottle / Cosmos Literary Agency, 32 Tynedale Avenue, Wallsend, Tyne and Wear, NE28 9LS, England and Sean Wallace, 589 Park Hill Drive, Apt. 8, Fairlawn, OH 44333, USA, and printed and distributed by Lightning Print, a subdivision of Ingrams Book Group, USA. All purchase orders should be sent to Philip Harbottle (UK) and Sean Wallace (USA).

INTRODUCTION

WHEN English writer John Russell Fearn began selling science fiction stories to the American magazines in the early 1930s, he was the *only* full-time science fiction writer in the country. Accordingly, he pursued his chosen profession with intense dedication and vigour for many years. After the Second World War, he continued to write sf, but also diversified into other form of fiction, particularly detective and western fiction. Science fiction remained his first love, however, and during the last three years of his life, all of his later published works were science fiction novels for the Canadian general interest magazine, the Toronto *Star Weekly*.

Accordingly, for this first **Cosmos Books** edition of Fearn, I have chosen two stories carefully selected from his earliest and later writings. Neither story has ever appeared in book form, in keeping with the **Cosmos** policy of publishing only first editions.

From the early American sf magazines, I have selected the novelette **Creation's End**. The story was originally published in the June 1941 issue of *Science Fiction* as by "Thornton Ayre" under the title of **The World in Wilderness**, and was illustrated by Hannes Bok. This presentation was reprinted in the February 1942 issue of an ultra-rare Canadian magazine, also confusingly titled *Science Fiction* (but which used selected reprints from several magazines from the same U.S. publishing stable.) Both these wartime publications are now rare, particularly the Canadian magazine, which most modern collectors have never even heard of, let alone seen! The story is therefore something of a "lost classic" and in restoring it to print under Fearn's own name, it also seemed appropriate to restore Fearn's original evocative working title of **Creation's End**.

Lacking a scientific education – like most of his contemporaries, Fearn had been obliged to leave school at 14 and seek employment – the author set out to educate himself in the sciences. He became an assiduous reader and collector of scientific text books. His personal reference library contained an astonishing range of scientific treatises on anthropology, astronomy, chemistry, meteorology, physics, and so forth. Because his early work appeared in "pulp" magazines, successive sf historians and commentators, swallowing the "perceived wisdom" without reading his stories, have dismissed Fearn as an unscientific slam-bang action story writer. This is far from the truth.

Perhaps the two most famous scientist-authors in the 1930s were Sir James Jeans and Sir Arthur Eddington – the Stephen Hawkings of their day. Fearn was fascinated by their books on cosmogony, as both authors exercised their imaginations to the full, and were not afraid to speculate on the still-unknown properties of space and time. In particular, Fearn was fascinated by Jeans' evocatively-titled *The Mysterious Universe*, published in 1930. Jeans was one of the earliest and most persuasive proponents of the "tidal theory" of the creation of the solar system. Many pre-war scientists believed that the immense gravitational forces exerted by the passage of a runaway star close to our sun had wrenched out a stream of solar matter, which had then cooled and condensed into the planets of our solar system. It was an intensely exciting and romantic notion, and Fearn based several of his early sf stories around it. They included *The Blue Infinity* (1935), *The Cosmic Juggernaut* (1940) and *The World In Wilderness* (1941). In reprinting the latter story (as **Creation's End**) we offer modern readers a fascinating glimpse into both scientific and science fiction history.

Manton's World was originally published as "The Novel of the Week" in *The Star Weekly* for June 9, 1958 – two days after Fearn's 50th birthday. It has never been reprinted. *The Star Weekly* was (and still is) one of Canada's largest selling magazines, with a paid circulation well in excess of 900,000 copies, but it was *not* a science fiction magazine. Rather, it was a slick tabloid general interest magazine. Its magazine section contained a centre-page newspaper supplement, consisting of famous American comic strip characters like "Tarzan" and "L'il

Abner" and inside the comics section was printed a "Complete Novel." *The Star Weekly* was a prestigious high-paying market, and attracted authors of international renown, such as Hermina Black, John Dickson Carr, Erle Stanley Gardner, Berkeley Gray, Charles L. Hecklemann, Archie Joscelyn, Philip MacDonald, Ellery Queen, Roy Vickers – and even P.G.Wodehouse! In keeping with its general appeal (many of its readers were Canadian housewives) most of the novels used were detective stories, westerns, and romances. During his lifetime, Fearn was in fact the *only* science fiction author to be regularly featured: a unique distinction. Paradoxically, despite the magazine's huge circulation, like all of the weekly novels issued as special supplements, Fearn's *Star Weekly* novels are also ultra-rare, and unknown to collectors. Few copies seem to have survived – almost certainly due to their awkward size and ephemeral tabloid newspaper format.

Fearn died suddenly and unexpectedly from a heart attack in September 1960, having just completed his final work, *Earth Divided* (a Golden Amazon novel). It was published posthumously by *The Star Weekly*, and in response to intense reader demands (and with the agreement of Fearn's widow) the *Star* commissioned the Scott Meredith Literary Agency to find another writer to continue the Amazon series. Many famous sf writers were tried out...*but all of them were rejected!* None of these specialist sf magazine writers could duplicate Fearn's unique "popular" style. As previously noted, Fearn had been the *only* sf writer to be published by the *Star* Syndicate, which licensed reprints to at least four newspapers in the Maine and New York areas. This vast readership were not sf "buffs" and required entertaining fiction told in understandable human terms – a quite different approach to the material appearing in the specialist sf magazines.

Although **Manton's World** deals with recognisable science fiction archetypes and tropes – the aftermath of an atomic war, mutants, space travel, aliens, and the threat of global catastrophe – these themes are treated as subsidiary to a story of human interest. At times distinctly unscientific (even in 1958 Fearn knew perfectly well that human-type life on Venus was an impossibility) and naïve, the story is beguilingly deceptive. It

manages to touch on a number of profound philosophical and
sociological issues – the misuse of science, ecology and the
balance of nature, racism, and the conflict between youth and
maturity – to name but a few – without the slightest hint of
didacticism or slackening of narrative interest. Fearn's appeal is
best summarised by the noted Italian critic and sf publisher Ugo
Malaguti: "...with his apparent simplicity of message, he
manages to concentrate into ten lines the fears, the hopes, and
dynamism of dozens of pages of other writers' work. This is the
real reason for his success, and the reason why, as a writer, he
is destined never to die."

Philip Harbottle,
Wallsend,
September, 1999.

CHAPTER ONE

The big fellow stood on a high ridge overlooking what had once been a city. Beside him stood a young woman of perhaps his own age. She held tightly to the hand of a girl of six, as though she was afraid to let her go. To right, left, and rear of the ridge were churned and battered fields, still issuing sulphuric-looking smoke.

"Once," said the big man, pointing, "that was a proud city. Now it is an ash heap. Once there was a London on the map. Now it is only a memory. Does one good to remember that now and again."

"Yes," Ann, his wife, acknowledged quietly. "Does one good. But little more than that. They'll be at it again the moment they have the chance. You men will never learn."

The big fellow turned. He was nearing 30. His physique was massive, produced mainly by the army training he had received for seven merciless years.

"What do you mean by 'you men'?" he asked Ann bluntly. "It is obvious from that that you include me among them."

Ann smiled colorlessly. "I do. You're a man, aren't you? You have the same strain as all men. If there is a chance to dominate, you'll take it. I haven't been married to you all these years not to know that."

"Sit down, Ann. There's something you ought to know about my intentions in this new world."

Ann shrugged and squatted on the slag heap with the youngster beside her. Randle Manton sat too, his powerful forearms hanging over his upthrust knees. It did not matter for any of them that the slagheap was dirty. Their clothes were little better than rags, anyway.

"We're at the end of our age and the beginning of another," Manton said, after a moment. "Everybody has had their fill of war and squabbling because this seven-year packet has reduced the world to rubble and left precious few survivors. Those survivors are dead against war and power-politics, and I'm one of them.

We've learned a lot of things from the war, as one always does. The boost to science has been tremendous and discoveries have been made which ordinarily never would have been made."

"The filth of war will always stay with us as an ineraseable stain," Ann whispered, tears in her eyes. "That stain will always be on Elise..." Her arm went around the child protectively. "She was spared to us, I know, but at a price. Perhaps it would have been better if radiation had killed her. Better perhaps than leaving her as she is."

Manton tightened his mouth, his mind flashing back to the night when Elise had been born. The atomic war had been in full blast then. He had been miles away. Elise was born safely enough, but atomic radiation did its work just the same, and the one faculty the child had not got was sight.

"Try to forget it," Manton said quietly. "At least she did not develop into one of these ghastly Mutants which are all too prevalent. At least she looks like you or me, instead of a crazy travesty of a human being."

Ann did not say anything. She looked out toward the ruins of London and thought her own thoughts... Away in the distance was the encampment from which she, her husband, and Elise had come —a crude affair amid thousands of similar dwellings; a patched up arrangement of bricks, corrugated iron sheets, and tarpaulin which was called home.

At a sudden sound Ann looked up, and almost immediately looked away again. A man in rags and tatters was moving nearby, searching for firewood. He held by the hand a mutant child, about the same age of Elise, a big-headed monstrosity with arms twice the normal length. Atomic radiation had done this to the mother before the child had been born. There were hundreds of them down in the encampment.

"There are times," Manton whispered, "when I'm glad Elise cannot see this world she's come into. There may be mercy in the fact that a screen is drawn over it all—at least until some kind of order and decency is produced from it all. And that is my task, and men like me."

"What do you think you can do?" Ann asked at last. "One man alone?"

"I don't propose to work alone; no man could do that. But I do intend to talk to other men of the same ideas, and between us we'll try and sort ourselves out. Start civilisation going again...start, maybe, a Golden Age."

Ann smiled sadly, almost hopelessly. Then she turned as the child at her side spoke.

"Mummy, what's a Mutant?"

"You wouldn't understand, dear. It's something horrible."

"You and daddy have been saying such a lot about Mutants. Do they look like—like I suppose I look?"

"Never in this world, my love—never!" Ann replied, clutching the child to her and kissing her. "You are as a little girl should look. Sweet and—altogether adorable. And a Mutant is—is something you shouldn't know about."

Elise smiled—a round, cherubic smile—and her big, yet blank gray eyes searched around in the darkness for a moment.

"I'm glad I'm not a Mutant," she said. "You wouldn't love me if I was."

Manton passed a big hand over his face and sat for a moment as though shielding the dark sun from his eyes.

"I must talk to the people this evening," he said. "If we are going to make some definite moves—and we certainly are—we must make them before the winter comes. Which won't be very long now. We're already in late August. I think we'll arrange something. This present rocky interim post-war government we've got wants abolishing. Six months they have been in power and they haven't done anything useful."

"Restoring things after seven years of atomic war cannot be too easy," Ann said. "We haven't given them much time yet."

"They've had time enough!" Suddenly and decisively Manton got to his feet. "They want a man of action—and they've got one..."

He held down a great hand to help Ann rise. She did so, then Manton stooped and swept little Elise up against his huge shoulder.

"Time we were getting back," he said. "In fact, it's time for lots of things..."

He started to move resolutely, the youngster tightly held in one arm. Silent and gray-faced Ann followed behind him down the ashy, rubble-strewn slope.

The "Encampment" where the Mantons had their home, stretched over the original heart of London and looked rather like the one-time slums. Actually it was fairly well run, and all matters of sanitation had been thoroughly dealt with. There was a supply of cold water to each dwelling, and electric light was promised for the future. Meantime there were oil lights. The Encampment boasted two schools—one for normal children and one for Mutants, since both required a distinct type of training—a small place of worship, and a scattering of buildings which served as stores.

That evening, even as he had told Ann, Manton made his way to the centre of the Encampment, where the people usually assembled after sundown, and began to talk to them. They listened, chiefly because Manton was a good talker, and also because he knew what he was talking about. In the flickering green light of mercury vapor lamps—the best lighting which could be contrived for exterior illumination—he gathered around him quite a small audience as the time wore on. Both men and women were interested.

"We have everything in our favor," Manton insisted. "Among you men here there are engineers, architects, railroad experts, highway designers, builders—everything. At the moment we are just drifting along under an emergency government, and we shall continue to drift for the simple reason that the government doesn't know where to turn amongst this rubble in order to make a fresh start. If any start is to be made we must make it—now! Before we grow too lethargic."

The people looked at him in silence, a towering giant of a man with threadbare clothes and a brown, swarthy skin. Every part of him radiated power and leadership. He was definitely the man of destiny for his time, a man appointed to jerk the weary, war-sick survivors into action in spite of themselves.

"For yourselves you may not think the effort to rebuild is worthwhile," Manton continued. "If that be so, then bury your selfishness and think instead of the young ones who will have to make something of this shambles which our generation has created. Give them a chance to having something worthwhile. Most of you here have sons and daughters of school-age. Some are Mutants, who will need special care to adapt themselves to the world to come. Others are handicapped in other ways through the curse of atomic radiation—like my own daughter who has been blind since birth. To them we owe something, otherwise we will fail in our duty as parents."

At least Manton had made a start. The more he talked, the more he had the people behind him, and when he finally ceased it was with the promise to return to the same spot the following night with some kind of ordered plan properly outlined. He arrived at his own dwelling in a more light-hearted mood than he had known since the war had ended.

"Well?" Ann said quietly. "How did you get on?"

"Perfectly." He hugged her shoulders. "Definite move in the right direction! Tomorrow we'll really get some action—when I have drafted out plans for what I intend to do."

"What do you intend to do?"

"Rebuild London, of course. That's the first thing. After that we'll reach out to rebuild other cities. We can gain a monopoly over building materials, atomic power for lighting and heating our dwellings. Dozens of things too complicated for you to understand."

"I can understand that you are arranging things so that you will have the control of them."

"You don't object to my taking control, surely?"

"No; provided you will know where to stop. Men such as you, Randle, with unbounded ambition, create wars without realizing it. The first challenge to your authority will bring trouble."

"I'm sorry you look at it that way," he said quietly. "But I'm going on, just the same. If only for her sake."

He glanced toward the rough bed where Elise was lying fast asleep. Ann looked too, and shrugged. Then she came over and poured out a cup of tea.

"Don't misunderstand me, Randle. I'm not saying you shouldn't try and improve our lot. That's got to be done. But if you gain a little authority, will you be content with just that, or will you seek to gain even greater authority, no matter what? Too much authority of the ruthless kind leads to wars, and we know what war leads to! I'm just uneasy for you, Randle."

"Then don't be!" Manton clutched her to him again, possessively, with that iron strength he possessed. With fierce impulse, he kissed her.

"I wouldn't think much of you as a wife if you didn't look out for my interests," he grinned. "But you're worrying needlessly. I am thinking of building up a powerful position for myself—remember I'm not even 30 yet—and then I want to manoeuvre myself into a spot whereby I can get enough money together to have Elise put right. I'll go to any length to get that."

"Isn't that chasing a rainbow, dear?" Ann sighed. "Elise is beyond cure. The doctors who've seen her have told us so."

"Ordinary doctors, yes. I'm thinking of scientific experts who deal in advanced means of curing all sorts of things. The experts who've popped up all over the place during the war."

"Yes, dear. Your tea's getting cold."

Randle Manton grunted and swallowed a mouthful; then a sudden thought seemed to strike him. He stared in front of him for a moment.

"Say, that's funny!"

"What? The tea? Haven't I—"

"No—not the tea. You were saying a moment ago about chasing rainbows. When did you last see one?"

Ann screwed up her eyes and thought. "Must be before the war. I don't recall seeing one during the actual war itself—but then the skies were mostly smoke-palled anyhow."

"Not all the time. I've seen the sky often after a shower—or rather with the rain still falling and sun behind the rain yet there's been no rainbow... There should have been one, come to think of it. Solar spectrum reflected."

"To me it seems like the withdrawal of a promise," Ann said, slowly getting to her feet and thinking. "God promised that the rainbow was the sign that He would never again flood the world. And now the sign has gone."

Manton laughed. "You and your Bible! I'm not making mock, my love, but in this case there is probably a scientific reason for the disappearance of rainbows. Radioactive dust interfering with the spectrum, maybe..."

He returned to his supper, leaving Ann thinking. Queer about rainbows. She wondered why she had never noticed it before.

CHAPTER TWO

Without making any particular effort Randle Manton soon had the support of every man and woman in the Encampment, and from that moment onwards it was more or less a matter of natural development plus hard work which laid a new civilization on the ruins of the old.

In two years the Encampment was done away with and upon its site grew the new centre of London—a streamlined version of the old reaching more up than across with the result that skyscrapers were the main feature topped by aircraft landing bases and private helicopter parking grounds. Down below in the canyons of masonry and steel, bridges linked the buildings, some carrying vehicles and others for pedestrians.

Central among these buildings stood Manton's own headquarters—Manton's Enterprises Incorporated.—which included pretty well everything which worked at a profit. Manton's Enterprises were just at the beginning of their career and Randle Manton himself, as the managing director, was quite certain what course he was going to take. With his finger on the pulse of the profit-making commercial enterprises of the day he failed to see how he could miss.

In five years he had extended his influence over most of the rebuilt country and in 10 years his financial and commercial genius was throwing out feelers into other lands. Randle Manton was everywhere, either under his own name or under an alias. In the tenth year one of his greatest coups was to swing the television and radio companies to his banner, which gave him unlimited power to advertise.

In private life, Ann Manton had little to really complain about. Randle gave her all she wanted. Elise, now 16, determined not to allow her handicap to make her a liability, had become a skilled telephonist in the Central London Exchange. She did her job the same way as any other worker and never for the moment sought to cash in on the fact that she was Randle Manton's daughter.

On the face of it, the new civilisation was happy enough—but nobody knew better than Randle Manton that this was purely the surface aspect. There was one strong undercurrent which, so far, he had not managed to stifle, and it was growing in strength, too. The undercurrent called itself the Union of the Young, with a dynamic young man named Nicholas Chauncey at its head. The Unions' sole purpose for existing, it appeared, was to ensure a square deal for the south of the country which up to now it did not seem to have had—and Randle Manton was blamed for the fact.

At first he endeavored to brush it aside as of no consequence, but it wasn't so easy as that. Nicholas Chauncey was a very determined young man and he meant to be heard—as Manton found out one morning when Chauncey was permitted to see him at his headquarters.

Manton sat at his desk appraising the young man and trying to decide whether he liked him or not. He was aged about 22, had an upstanding thatch of red hair, and a pugnacious mouth and short nose. Yet there was something so cheerfully impudent about him that he had an appeal in a vague kind of way.

"Glad to meet you, Mr. Manton," he said, shaking hands. "I've been hoping for it for a long time."

Manton shrugged. "Now you've got your wish. What's on your mind?"

"Youth, Mr. Manton. Young men and women like myself—from the age of about 13 to 25. There are quite a lot of them in the country—in fact, in the world. And they will always be following on, of course."

"Naturally. What about them?"

"You haven't consulted them in regard to the rebuilding of civilization."

Manton stared for a moment then he laughed. "Oh, come now, Mr. Chauncey! You don't expect me to consult teenagers as to how I shall run things, do you?"

"The future belongs to us," Chauncey said quietly. "We want all laws revised. We don't want the regulations which have been made by our elders, and which have resulted in endless wars. We don't want in a few years to see the Earth turned into another battleground."

"It won't be," Manton said. "You have my assurance."

"Have I?" Chauncey raised a doubtful eyebrow. "What will you do when the struggle begins for control of the planets which surround us? You won't just sit tight you know. You'll see to it that at any cost Earth is the master of the situation and if the other planets' inhabitants don't like it and make war because of it you'd make war too. And so the merry-go-round will go on."

"You have some alternative plan?" Manton inquired.

"We had. We had plans for a new civilization altogether but you older ones got ahead of us and didn't give us the chance to speak. Now where are we? We have to wait for men to die before we can step into their shoes and all that time we are becoming older, too. We think you and others working beside you, cheated us out of our inheritance."

"What inheritance?" Manton asked, trying not to sound irritated.

"The Golden Age."

If Manton was surprised he did not show it. He reflected briefly that maybe his conception of a Golden Age was vastly different from that of Nicholas Chauncey.

"An age of security, with all the amenities of science to attend to our needs," Chauncey went on. "That is what science is for, properly controlled. To help us, not destroy us...You have built up a new civilization and are stretching your power right across the earth. For that, all credit, but the only people in your sphere of interest are those who were commencing to be big noises when the atomic war broke out. Now you've gathered together those still surviving and have given them positions of authority. It's all wrong! They're polluted with pre-war ideas, and for that very reason they'll sow the seeds of future disaster. You should have used young fresh minds with an entirely new outlook."

Manton considered for a moment, then he spread his hands.

"What do you suggest, Mr. Chauncey? The tearing down of everything we've built up since the war, and handing over control to you youngsters?"

"Handing over control—yes. Tearing everything down—no. What has been put up can have the necessary modification. Sounds like a crazy idea, doesn't it? But then, youth has always been labelled as crazy."

"And small wonder!" Manton snapped. "Have your pipe dreams somewhere else, Mr. Chauncey, and stop carrying a torch for a gang of irresponsible in-betweens."

Chauncey remained unshaken by the blast. He moved toward the door.

"You'll hear more of me, Mr. Manton, and of the Union of the Young. We're not without money or numbers, and we mean to get what we're out for. This new world is a youngsters' world, and we don't intend to have it governed by men and women who are already on the decline!"

The door closed decisively and for a few moments Manton sat staring blankly before him. In all his experience he had never come across a young man like Nicholas Chauncey. He didn't like it. It left a nasty taste in his mouth.

Meanwhile, Nick Chauncey returned through the labyrinth of the city to the modest headquarters of the Union of the Young. When he entered the building he found it pretty well packed with young people of all ages from 13 to 25. Some were Mutants, but by common agreement they were treated as equal to the Normals. That was one invariable law of the union—that all were equal.

As Chauncey entered there was brief silence; then questions suddenly broke out. Chauncey did not answer any of them. Instead he went to the raised dais at the end of the room and put up a hand for silence.

"Just a minute, all of you. Let me speak and fire your questions afterwards. I've seen Randle Manton, as I promised you I would, and I got exactly nothing out of the interview. Rather as I had expected, he looks upon us as a joke."

"I don't suppose that's very surprising," a young physicist sighed. "Naturally, like all men at his age, he regards youth as a necessary evil entirely unsuited to have power in its hands."

"Then his opinion must be changed," Chauncey said flatly. "We must show him by example that we are fully capable of responsibility. I happen to know that space travel is now a worthwhile project—it developed tremendously during the war—and will be one of the first things Manton will seize upon. Cheap atomic power will make it an economic proposition. Our boys know exactly which financiers are willing to back a space corporation and my suggestion is that we step in before Manton does."

For a moment there was an astonished silence.

"You serious?" asked a girl biologist.

"Of course I'm serious; and I'm prepared to visit the necessary financiers and scientists to arrange a deal, if I have the approval of a majority of our members."

Again the suggestion of doubt. Chauncey could smell it in the air.

"Well, what's the matter with you?" he demanded. "We want a giant's stride to show that we can handle modern business, and here I am offering you the chance. Yet you hesitate? Why?"

The physicist who had first spoken got to his feet. "I think we all have the feeling that that would be a project too large for us to handle. Space travel of all things!"

"All right, all right," Chauncey said, raising his hands. "It comes down to this: Space travel will come, and quickly. If older people will be able to handle it, why can't we? That's all there is in the issue. Give me a vote of confidence and let me go ahead."

There was a pause as the secretary to the union made a brief estimate of the number of members present. Finally he decided that it constituted a majority, upon which a vote was taken. It ended in agreement for Chauncey's suggestion and, smiling to himself, he left the dais and descended into the body of the hall. For a time he found himself involved in answering questions from one or other of the members, Mutants among them, then he turned aside as a slim, fair-haired girl with a pretty face touched his arm.

"You're Nick Chauncey?" she asked, in a quiet, soft voice.

"Certainly," Nick grinned. "Isn't the red hair and sawn-off nose distinctive enough?"

"I wouldn't know," Elise Manton smiled. "I'm blind."

Nick started a little, looking into her wide gray eyes. Though they were looking at him they were also looking into space.

"I'm sorry," Nick said quietly. "Very sorry."

"You don't have to be; I get along all right. I'd rather like a word with you, Mr. Chauncey."

"Surely. And drop out the prefix, please. I'm Nick to everybody in the union."

"Okay, then. Shall we go somewhere quiet?"

Nick nodded and took her arm, leading her into a quiet part of the hall. He settled her on one of the chairs and then waited.

"I've been a member of the union for some time because I believe in its aims," Elise said, after a moment. "By occupation I'm a telephonist, and since I'm on late shift I was able to come this morning. I know you object to the way Randle Manton is running things, and I know you think could do it much better—as you probably could. But I think you'll waste your time in trying out this space corporation project."

"Why?" Nick asked bluntly. "If we don't try, we'll never know."

"In that I agree; but if you'll believe me let me tell you something. Space travel control will fall into your lap like a ripe plum if you'll only wait long enough. In that way you won't need to antagonize Randle Manton and bring the whole of the union into disrepute."

Nick moved impatiently. "I'm afraid you're not making much sense. You say Manton will create a space corporation, and yet you say it will fall into our hands, like a ripe plum if we wait. I can see that happening! Once Manton gets his hand on things he'll stick to them... What possible grounds can you have for talking as you do?"

"I have the gift of second sight," Elise answered quietly; then added, "On numerous occasions I've proved this sense to be correct. Maybe it is nature's compensation to me; maybe it is something produced in my mind by atomic bomb blast. I don't know. But it's there. If you'll be guided I can help you tremendously, not only now but the future."

"I'm afraid I don't have any faith in fortune tellers," Nick said reluctantly.

"There's a difference between fortune-telling and being psychic, Nick."

"I'm sorry. I didn't quite mean it that way. Even so, I shall have to go through with it after all I've had to say to the union. I can't possibly back out." Nick looked at the girl's thoughtful profile keenly. "You never know. You may have guessed wrong."

"This isn't a matter of guesswork, Nick. It's a matter of knowing. The visions are only infrequent, but they never lead me astray."

"Which suggests there is a difference between visions and hallucinations," Nick said. "Sorry, I didn't mean to offend you, Miss—What is your name, by the way?"

"Elise Manton."

Elise could almost guess Nick's thoughts in the dead silence which followed. When at length he spoke his voice was coldly polite and uncompromising.

"Relative of Randle Manton, presumably?"

"I'm his daughter."

"I thought so. I seem to remember hearing somewhere that he has a blind daughter.... It no longer seems odd to me that you should wish me to give up the idea of forming a space corporation. Naturally, you want your father to get there first."

"Nothing of the kind." Elise felt for Nick's hand and gripped it tightly. "I've been a member of this union for a year now, Nick, and I strongly approve of most of its aims. I don't agree with my father in everything, particularly in some of his business deals. I don't care whether he gets the space corporation formed or not. I'm simply telling you to wait."

"And what about your father? Are you going to tell him that no matter what he does the space corporation will fall into our hands like a ripe plum?"

"No." Elise shook her head slowly. "I tried on two occasions to warn him on business matters, but he simply pooh-poohed the idea. The fact that later events proved me right made no difference. He put it down to coincidence.... I shall not warn him again, for the simple reason that he will not believe."

Nick detached the hand grip gently and got to his feet.

"Sorry, Miss Manton," he said quietly. "As I said before, I'll have to make an attempt after all I have said... Thanks just the same for the warning."

"I shall usually be in the union audience if at any time you want to talk to me," Elise answered, her empty gray eyes upon him.

For a moment Nick hesitated, feeling there was something he ought to add. Then as nothing occurred to him he shrugged and turned away.

CHAPTER THREE

The guided missile, new developments in atomic propulsion, a sure means of insulating man from its harmful radiations, and above all a crying need for more room and bigger trade areas all provided the basis for a demand that man travel into space. Newspapers began to clamor about it, the Manton television and radio circuits never stopped talking about it, the scientists said it was now quite a logical development—and financiers sniffed at it as a possible tasty morsel.

So Randle Manton himself acted. With all his other world pursuits functioning according to plan, with the octopus tentacles of his money power reaching out into every land, he decided it was time to look at this new development before somebody else beat him to it. That he heard vague rumors of somebody actually trying to do this was probably the spur to his ambitions.

He summoned five of the greatest financiers of the new world to his headquarters, along with the most reputable scientists, and proceeded to nail the matter to the boardroom table.

"It would seem, gentlemen," he said, when the preliminaries were over, "that Mr. and Mrs. Citizen are demanding a road to the stars—and therefore they must have it, at a profit to ourselves."

"A very good profit, if I may say so," one of the financiers grinned.

"First—you gentlemen." Manton looked at the scientists. "Am I to understand that space travel on a commercial basis is now practical?"

Brailsford, head of AEPU—Atomic Energy for Peaceful Uses —gave a nod.

"There may be fortunes on other worlds: there may be nothing." Brailsford said frankly. "We just don't know until we get there."

"I believe," Manton continued, turning again to the scientists, "that one of you gentlemen has drawn up a design for a spaceship, operating on the lowest possible power margin commensurate with the safety of the passengers?"

Sedberg, the rocket designer and engineer, opened up his brief case and spread a series of complicated designs on the table.

"There it is, Mr. Manton. I would place the cost of building the vessel at something like 750,000 credits."

"Three-quarters of a million for each vessel is not chicken feed," one of the financiers grunted.

Sedberg shrugged. "It cannot be done on less. And while I am about it I think I should remark that you are not the only men who would like to embark on this space project. I'm in the happy position that, if you finally refuse to do anything about it, I still have an eager client. One who will be willing to use my type of vessel and who'll make few bones about the cost."

"Who?" Manton looked up, his brows darkening. "Just who? Or is this some kind of blackmail, Mr. Sedberg, to force the issue?"

"Not blackmail, I assure you," Sedberg said. "And in honor bound I must preserve the name of the interested party."

"Would it be Chauncey?" asked one of the financiers bluntly. "That hothead who runs the Union of the Young?" Then as Sedberg remained silent the financier went on, "He tackled me, too, and some of you other boys, I believe. Said he had everything worked out and only wanted us to put up the money... I soon told him!"

"Yes, it was Nicholas Chauncey," Sedberg admitted. "A very pushing and enterprising young man. He couldn't name anybody who was willing to put up the money, so of course I couldn't do business with him... I don't want to disagree with you gentlemen, but I think young Chauncey has some very good ideas if he were given the chance to develop them."

"Young upstart," Manton growled. "All he wants is nothing less than control of the country while we older ones take a back seat."

"Shall we get back to the matter on hand?" Sedberg suggested mildly—and for the moment brought the topic of Nicholas Chauncey to a close. Indeed there began at that moment one of the long, cigar-smoking, wrangling sessions which were dear to Manton's heart. In the midst of the stuffy atmosphere he was the master of argument and had a ready answer for every difficulty. There was only a short break for lunch, then the conference resumed and persisted well into the afternoon.

Towards 4 o'clock Manton was glowing with satisfaction. He had not left any loopholes through which his financial colleagues could logically escape.

"Right!" Manton said. "We know exactly what we are doing, and I will call for tenders immediately. When we have them we'll go further. Factories will need building, the space port must be constructed, and men will be needed for pilots—and young women as space hostesses." Manton considered for a moment. "The last part should be easy. I'll get thc government to issue a conscription order. That will save all the uncertainty of volunteers."

"Don't you think that's a bit high-handed?" Sedberg asked.

Manton grinned. "Of course it is! But at least it will show Nicholas Chauncey and his romping youngsters where they stand. Do 'em good to have to serve the community. We'll want special types for pilots and hostesses, and they're the type the government will conscript. Leave it to me. I'll fix it."

*   *   *

Manton did everything he set out to do, because that was his way. The factories for spaceship construction were in various parts of the country, extremely hush-hush and constantly guarded. Working in liaison with the government, most of whose members— and even the prime minister himself—were personal friends of Manton, it had not been a difficult job to secure the necessary legislation for the conscription of "space workers" from the ranks of youth. These were now being trained, whether they liked it or not in various commandeered buildings for the work they would presently have to do. By and large, everything was going exacty as Manton wanted.

In between times Manton dabbled with the idea of climatic control, puzzling meanwhile on the almost constant cloud cover which seemed to blanket the earth in these post-war days. Climatic control was easily possible, according to the scientists, but against it was the usual lack of capital. Even Manton knew when he had to stop. There was enough finance involved already without adding anything more.

"Perhaps later on," he said to the meteorologist whom he had summoned to his office in order to get the facts. "I think the institution of world climatic control would be a good thing—not to say a profitable one."

"No doubt of it, sir," the weather man agreed. "It might serve to clear up the cloud blanket over the world. I frankly say that we can't understand why there should be constant cloud anyway unless it be a hangover from the war."

"After 10 years?" Manton exclaimed, and the meteorologist nodded.

"It's possible, Mr. Manton. During the war there were enormous discharges from atomic bombs for one thing. Though the radioactive dust has been rendered harmless it is still there, drifting to high altitudes and forming a thin screen which constantly—or nearly constantly—blocks the sunlight. There are days when diffused sunlight gets through, but they're rare."

"Climatic control would disperse all this?"

"I imagine so, sir. I'd know better if detailed study were made of the cloud screen, then we'd know what we're up against. It's certainly a very high screen. No airplane has yet got above it, so it must be set pretty close to the limit of earth's atmosphere."

"Must be," Manton acknowledged. "However, we'll know a good deal more when the space corporation gets going. We can have experts view the cloud cover from outer space and find out all about it. Then maybe we can go into the matter of climatic control more thoroughly."

"Up to you, Mr. Manton. Right now it looks as though earth is following the example of Venus in masking its face with eternal cloud."

"Yes, I suppose it does. Quite an interesting coincidence. It occurs to me that you might be the right man to study these weather conditions at first hand, so when the times comes for a study to be made I'll get in touch with you. You'd be prepared to take on the job?"

"Willingly, sir."

"Right. I shan't forget you."

With that the weatherman went on his way, and Manton turned back to his work, chiefly upon the details of the charges which would be made for the forthcoming space flights. That same evening a tentative schedule of the prices was telecast to an interested public—to the fury of one Nicholas Chauncey. That same evening, not an hour later, he made the reason for his anger known to an almost full gathering of the Union of the Young.

"Something's got to be done!" he declared flatly. "As if it isn't bad enough to have Randle Manton running everything his way the public has even got to be robbed when it comes to using this new medium of space flight. Have any of you seen these ticket prices?" he demanded, raising an evening paper in the air.

"Yes," somebody acknowledged, "but we can't do anything about it. Manton's entitled to charge what he likes, seeing as he controls the corporation. He's managing director, isn't he?"

"And a thief as well!" Chauncey retorted, his red hair bristling. "These prices prove it."

"I object to that!" Elise Manton got suddenly to her feet, her voice coldly challenging. "Whatever else my father may be, he is not a thief, and you've no right to say such a thing."

Nick tightened his mouth. "With all due respect. Miss Manton, I'm not making a wild statement. The charge here, for the return journey to Mars, is given as 2,000 credits. Two thousand! Could anything be more ridiculous?"

"I have not the least doubt," Elise said, "that my father knew what he was doing when he worked out the figures. You don't expect to carry a passenger over—say, 80 million miles of space, the distance there and back from Mars, for a few credits, do you?"

"Certainly not, but this is beyond all reason."

The assembly waited with interest for the reply. Passages at arms between the blind girl and the tough Nick Chauncey were a matter of course these days, for though disagreeing with her father's methods in many ways, Elise was at least loyal to him as his daughter.

"You seem to forget," Elise continued, "that these trips will demand colossal overheads to the corporation!"

"I said I didn't make my statements wildly," Nick interrupted. "There is no reason why a passenger should not travel to Mars and back for 500 credits return. Even then there'd be a profit."

Elise laughed slightly. "I'd like to see you run a space line on those figures, Mr. Chauncey!"

"That," Nick said deliberately, "is just what I intend to do!"

There was a puzzled silence for a moment. Elise, plainly stumped, felt for her chair and slowly sat down. In grim silence Nick surveyed the assembly for a moment.

"I said something has got to be done," he continued. "And it is going to be! Randle Manton has conscripted me and several other young men out of the Union, as space pilots. We've raised objections to such arbitrary methods, but they haven't got us anywhere. It's quite plain that Manton has done it to show us that he's the boss of the situation, and that we must do as we're told. All right, but if he thinks he's beaten us completely he's vastly mistaken."

"A moment!" one of the young women exclaimed. "Hadn't you better take care what you're saying, Nick, with Manton's own daughter right among us?"

Nick said: "When Elise Manton joined the Union of the Young she made several solemn promises. One of them was not to ever betray the confidences of the Union. Because I believe Elise is a girl of her word I shall go on talking, confident that she will not betray a single word of what I'm going to say, even though she is Manton's daughter."

"Quite right." Elise replied quietly. "I have a deep respect for this Union—I might even say an affection. and the promises I made I shall keep. Just one question, and it has nothing to do with the fact that I'm Randle Manton's daughter. I'd ask anyway.... Why do you want to smash his space line? Is it spite, revenge for his conscription order or what? It smacks all through of—retaliation."

"It isn't...and here's why. Your father is starting off on the wrong foot by profiteering to begin with. If he gets away with it he'll go one better—and so will lots of other men with him. It will lead to the grasping struggle for power that brought down the civilization before this one. And the one before that, almost. The Young People just won't stand for it anymore, and we're pledged to smash all grasping, profiteering concerns right at the start. A reasonable margin of profit is all that is needed. Fair dealing all round. Your father is not doing that... Further, when he reaches out to the other planets there will be the matter of control of those worlds, the bargaining for minerals and valuable ores. Manton is not the man to handle that. He is too ambitious. It demands a person or preferably a group of persons, who put the masses before themselves.... Does that answer your question?"

"Well, I'll accept it," Elise said enigmatically, and sat down again.

"There's something else," another pointed out. "You talk of forming this rival company, Nick. Okay—can you? Aren't you going to get into hot water duplicating a Sedberg spaceship? Both Manton and Sedberg himself will take legal action to restrain you."

"I don't intend duplication. I intend a modified version of the Sedberg model, different enough to prevent me being cited as a copyist. The lads among us who have made engineering and aeronautics their profession will deal with that. I've got it all worked out."

With that Nick descended into the hall and began answering a battery of various questions. Finally he found himself up against Elise. She had drifted through the main group and he first became aware of her by her light touch on his arm.

"Sorry, Nick, if I had a row with you," she apologized. "But I have my views and you have yours."

"Naturally," he agreed frankly. "Everything all clear now, or is there something else we should squabble over?"

"I was rather hoping we could forget 'business' for a bit and have a sort of chat—off the cuff. I always seem to be hearing the aggressive Nick Chauncey raging against my father and proclaiming the aims of the Union. I should imagine there is another Nick Chauncey somewhere, only it's not easy for me to find it. A normal girl has better advantages."

The girl turned her face toward him. For about the first time in the many weeks he had known her Nick studied her intently. She was definitely good-looking, with a straight nose and sweetly sensitive mouth. Her chin was remarkably determined, like that of her father, while the loosely caught fair hair betrayed the fact that she was still only 16. Her eyes, clear gray and large, never for an instant betrayed that there was no light in them.

"I'm surprised," Nick said, after a moment, "that with all the money he's got, your father doesn't do something to have your eyes put right. What kind of a father is he, anyway?"

"As a father I've no grumbles. The only thing I grumble about is his business life—and so does mother. Both of us are mortally afraid of him getting out of hand, and if he does there'll be the inevitable consequence of a war like the last one.... As for me, father has done all he can. Specialists and all sorts have examined me, and they're all quite sure nothing can be done. The optic nerves, and the portion of the brain responsible for sight were both paralyzed by bomb radiations a few weeks before I was born. I manage somehow, but at times..."

The girl's voice stopped and Nick saw her swallow hard.

"That isn't enough for me," he said. "Science has made vast strides, and will make even vaster ones. There'll be an answer to your troubles, perhaps sooner than you think."

"Thanks for the encouragement." Elise smiled faintly. "I'm not complaining too much. There were others born about the same time as myself who, today, are even worse off."

"That's no consolation to you, and I'll change it if I can..." Nick was silent for a moment, then: "You're not going to tell your father what I'm driving at in regard to a space line, are you?"

"You have my word, Nick."

"Good enough for me.... By the way, are you still sure that the space line is going to fall into our hands like a ripe plum?"

"Of course. It isn't just wishful thinking on my part: it's bound to happen. Only I don't know when. There's something else, too. As yet just a cloudy vision, but at times it is clearer. I've mentioned it to father, but as usual he's laughed at me. Now I'll mention it to you because I think you believe in me."

"I'll always believe in you, Elise."

"Well then, make what you can of this..." The girl frowned a little and stared hard into space. To Nick, watching her, it seemed that a stranger inner glow came to her eyes as she searched horizons beyond his vision. "It still isn't clear, but I can see a world different from any we have known. It isn't a vision of something beyond death. It's on this material plane, and it still is our world, but it's unrecognizeable. Water... I see it everywhere. The Earth is nearly a hydrosphere. I see rain, and rain and more rain. What it means, or when it will come, I can't say. But there it is."

"I believe it, though I can't understand it," Nick sighed—and for a long moment was quiet again. Then he glanced at his watch and quickly rose to his feet. "Sorry, Elise, I've got to be going. There's a night shift for space pilot training tonight. I have just time to see you home if you wish."

"No, no, I'll be all right." Elise rose beside him.

Nick hesitated, looking down at her. She was not as tall as he was. She was young—very young—and yet...

"I suppose this is taking advantage," he said. "I'm 22 and an enforced man of the world. You are only a girl and a good distance from being a woman—but some things are so powerful one cannot resist them."

Elise said nothing as he caught her almost fiercely in his arms and kissed her, not once but several times.

"That wasn't impulse," he said at last, hesitantly. "It wasn't something that I'll never do again. Maybe—in fact certainly—I'll do it again. The only thing that will stop me is you saying you don't wish me to.... Do you wish that?"

Elise stood, looking blankly toward the myriad lights of the city.

"No, Nick. I want you to do it—as often as you like. It makes me feel I'm wanted. That somebody really cares."

"Always, Elise—always."

Nick kissed her again, more gently this time. Then he released her slowly.

"I have to go," he said earnestly. "You do understand?"

"Yes, Nick. I understand."

And Elise stood silently listening to the retreat of his brisk foosteps.

CHAPTER FOUR

As far as Randle Manton could see, everything was perfect. The space corporation was functioning exactly as he had hoped it would, and pilots and hostesses were being trained in the dozens— by scientists under Sedberg's supervision. The spaceships themselves were coming off the production line with something like the regularity of automobiles.

By Christmas time the first batch of pilots were ready for action—Nick Chauncey among them. So far he had not resigned from the Manton Corporation. As yet he had not learned everything he wanted, and the day was drawing near when he would have to make the leap into space for research purposes. He received his first intimation of this from Manton himself in the big fellow's headquarters.

"I congratulate you, Mr. Chauncey, on having secured a first-class pilot's certificate," Manton said. "The Sedberg operatives tell me you are one of our best men, and in the future you will undoubtedly be one of our leading space pilots. A very handsome achievement for a fellow of 22."

"Yes, sir." Chauncey did not smile. He was coldly respectful and decidedly smart in his off-duty uniform.

"Three machines will be leaving Earth at 10 a.m. exactly a week from now. They will, if circumstances are favorable, make a round trip incorporating the moon, Mars and Venus. Each of these planets—though I suppose I ought to call the moon a satellite—is to be explored. The colonization possibilities, if any, are to be assessed by experts, and mineralogists will prepare reports on whatever minerals or ores are present on any of the three bodies. Naturally, a team of scientists will do that work. Your job will be to pilot the leading machine. In effect, you will be navigational leader of the expedition."

"Yes sir." Chauncey remained set-faced.

"You will take your orders from the scientists and go wherever they order. The expedition will take probably six months. By June next year, when the reports have been studied, the first passenger journeys can begin."

"I understand, sir. And what if Venus or Mars do not offer any possibilities? Do we extend the expedition to investigate the outer planets?"

"No. We'll have to examine the situation first. That's all, Mr. Chauncey. Final orders and details will reach you in due course."

Nick saluted and departed. That same evening he advised the Union of the Young that there was to be six months' wait before any definite action could be taken, six months in which he would learn all the final details he needed to know together with full information concerning the planets and their possibilities. By and large, at the moment the position suited him well enough.

"Six months will be a long time to wait," Elise sighed as they had supper together at a downtown restaurant.

"No choice," Nick said. "And anyway I'll find out everything I need to know, free of cost to myself. I've told Barker, my right-hand man, to keep in touch with events here that the thread won't be lost when I return to pick it up again. I've also asked him to have an eye to you. If ever you're in trouble, be sure to contact him."

Elise smiled. "I'll remember that."

"In the meantime, thanks for being loyal to the Union and saying nothing of my plans to your father."

"I never will. You have my word on that."

Nick continued wilh his supper for a moment and then he looked about him rather whimsically.

"Fourteen days to Christmas, Elise—and I shan't be here when the festive season comes. It's a queer thought. But I have a week which is as good as a holiday before take-off." He gripped the girl's wrists suddenly. "What do you say? Can't we cram every minute of it with fun? Forget the Union, forget future plans, forget everything except you and me. We're young and we're entitled... We haven't had much chance to find out what we'd like to know about each other."

"It's a wonderful idea!" Elise's cheeks colored a little. "I have seven days owing to me from the telephone exchange. I can take it whenever I want."

"Then start tomorrow," Nick decided. "For seven glorious days we'll paint the town red."

*   *   *

All too soon the week was over and the good-byes had been said. Nick received his final instructions and at 10 o'clock on the appointed morning stood in the control-room of the space machine which was to be the leader-ship of the expedition... In her home Elise was still in bed—her work shift not due to start for six hours —and she listened intently to the portable radio as every detail of the preliminaries and then the actual take-off was described.

The noise of that take-off she heard quite distinctly across the city without recourse to radio. A mounting, shattering whine that drowned out every other sound and then slowly faded into silence. It came again and again as the other ships took off until at last the quietness was a permanent thing.

Elise felt tears suddenly come into her eyes. For an awful moment she wondered if perhaps Nick would never return. It was only then that she realized how much she really loved him.

*   *   *

For Nick himself there were none of these thoughts: he had too much to do in the matter of hard concentration as he guided the spaceship into the airless void beyond the Earth. He would not have been human to not be impressed by the wonder of the achievement. With the other scientists in the control-room, he gazed upon the blacker-than-black void with its icy, unwinking stars, the prominence-girdled sun with its incredible corona, and the slowly receding Earth, the stars reaching to the pinkish band created by the atmosphere.

Yet there was an odd look about Earth, and it seemed to lie in the cloud formation—as distinct from the atmospheric envelope. It looked almost as though a faintly reflective cloud existed beyond the main cloud covering. A gigantic ring of cloud, going right around the Earth, and having something of the appearance of the rings of Saturn, though much nearer to Earth than the rings of

Saturn are to Saturn. It was an inescapable, mystifying phenomenon, which had been created by the atomic war.

Meredith, the weatherman, was the first to comment upon it. His interest in the formation was something more than that: it was an absolute fascination as he gazed through the big outlook port.

"That's got to be studied out carefully," he said, turning. "I never saw anything like it. Manton sent me on this trip to weigh up the possibilities of climatic stations down on Earth, and from the looks of things I'm going to have a decidedly amazing report."

Nick Chauncey, who, of course, took no part in the general scientific wranglings between the experts, nevertheless kept his ears open and learned a good deal. He learned plenty from Meredith, too—who was always willing to toss his theories around provided nobody accepted them as fact. Otherwise Nick stuck exclusively to his job and spent what little spare time he had in noting down details about the vessel, and its general construction.

CHAPTER FIVE

In mid-August, eight weeks behind the prescribed time, there came a faint resumption of signals from outer space; then they gradually grew stronger, and it dawned on an excited world that the expedition into space had been successful. The travellers were returning, and according to their own story they had been as far as Mars and Venus and done all they had set out to do.

Manton's interest in the radio reports was profound. He took time off from his various business interests to study the reports in detail. It was plain to him, long before the travellers reached Earth, that journeying into space would be possible. There were no inhabitants on either Mars or Venus, so those worlds were there for the taking, and everything they contained was the property of the Manton Space Corporation by reason of them being first there. On the lonely ochre deserts of Mars and the saturating supertropical regions of Venus the imprint of Manton had been made, in the shape of a silk flag.

So the travellers came back, and there followed interminable conferences with the scientists and the full Manton board of directors, as every detail was hammered out.

"It is rather remarkable to find that each one of you looks exactly the same as when you departed," Manton commented, when they were near the end of their conferences. "Somehow I had expected you to be changed. I even doubted if some of you would ever return at all."

"The machines themselves behaved perfectly," Sedberg said, with a quiet pride in his designing. "We didn't encounter any alien life or dangerous monsters, such as has often been suggested by imaginative writers, nor did we find the remains of any mighty civilizations. Venus and Mars are both empty worlds, so there won't be haggling with the governments of those worlds. We appropriated them, in the name of Earth."

"Splendid." There was a faraway look in Manton's eyes; then he turned his attention to the directors. "Well, gentlemen, I think our project shows distinct signs of turning in an enormous dividend. From the reports here on the moon it seems that there is precious metal in abundance, so obviously we must send mining engineers there almost the first thing we do. As for the tourist traffic, that can begin almost immediately. No prolonged stays to commence with, until we have erected the necessary hotels. But sightseers can be dealt with right now and we can start raking their money in."

"The machines to take them are finished?"

"Everything has been completed in the time you have been away," Manton responded. "There is nothing to stop our going into action right away."

Certainly there were still more details to complete, but by the end of August everything was ready. All the people of wealth and leisure—and inclination—were ready for the first venture into space in the luxurious Manton liners. Another batch of machines, of less elaborate design, had already gone on ahead to the moon to commence mining operations, and were not likely to be back for some time.

Then it was that the blow fell. Nick Chauncey, ready for this moment, refused his briefing orders at space headquarters and was immediately referred to Manton himself.

"And what is the meaning of this?" Manton demanded, as Nick stood before him. "Is this a strike, or what exactly is the situation?"

"It's not a strike, sir. It's complete withdrawal from the Manton space line. Every pilot and every space hostess. They all have orders from me to resign."

"Don't talk like an idiot!" Manton snapped, coloring. "You are a contracted employee of this company, and have been thoroughly trained. You can't suddenly back out in his fashion."

"I can, and I'm going to. The expeditionary flight was unpaid. It was considered part of my training. My salary would begin from now on, but it's not going to because I refuse to work for you. As long as I have not been paid, I am informed that, legally, I can do as I choose."

"We'll see about that! Don't you realize that there are hundreds of passengers waiting to..."

"I am aware of it, sir, but it makes no difference. The Union has decided to act on its own account, and I'm going to lead it."

"Act on its own account? Doing what, may I ask?"

"Establishing a second space line. We shall be a while getting things arranged, but it will certainly come. When it comes, Mr. Manton, be prepared for hard competition."

Manton got to his feet, his face set in craggy lines. "I was under the impression that the idiotic Union of the Young had died a natural death a long time ago, but evidently I was mistaken. I shall give orders for it to be broken up immediately, and every one of its members who are not employed by me as pilots or hostesses shall have a year in jail. Perhaps that will teach them sense."

"In that case," Nick shrugged. "I'm afraid you are going to miss your daughter an awful lot."

"My daughter!" Manton's eyes widened a little. "What exactly has she got to do with it?"

"Everything. She's been a member of the Union nearly since it began. If you lock up the members you'll have to include her, otherwise you'll be accused of favoritism. That won't go down well with anybody."

"I'm warning you, Chauncey—"

"I'll risk your warnings, and I'm quitting as from now."

With that Nick unclipped his official pilot's badge from his uniform and tossed it on the desk. Manton stared down at it incredulously, unable to grasp the fact that anybody—especially somebody as young as Nick Chauncey—should have the temerity to defy him. It was unheard of... When he looked up again the door was closing on Nick's departure.

Manton whipped up the telephone and spoke briefly. "Relay this message to the space grounds. Departure will be postponed for a few hours pending further statements... Also instruct the space ground police to prevent all pilots and hostesses from leaving the grounds. When they have done that, report back to me."

"Yes, Mr. Manton."

"Defy me, will he?" Manton muttered, putting the phone down again. "We'll see about that!"

He did not resume his seat at the desk: his mind was too disturbed by the sudden setback to permit him to concentrate. Instead he roamed around the gigantic office, a cigar speared between his strong teeth. At the jangling of the telephone he snatched it up again.

"Space ground police here, Mr. Manton."

"Well?" Manton demanded. "Have you carried out my orders?"

"I'm afraid we were not able to, sir. All the pilots and hostesses have disappeared from the grounds. It seems they went about half an hour ago, about the time Pilot Chauncey came to see you."

With a terrific effort Manton controlled himself. He bit hard on his cigar.

"Very well. I'll give you fresh instructions later. My other message was broadcast, I assume? That departure will be delayed?"

"Yes, sir."

Manton rang off and stared for a moment through the window at the distant view of the space grounds. The machines were lined up under the gray, misty sky, ready for the departure. Presumably they were filled to capacity with wealthy tourists who very soon would begin chafing with delay. Finally Manton made up his mind and summoned Sedberg, in charge of take-off, to his office.

The designer looked vaguely surprised as he came in.

"Anything wrong, Mr. Manton?"

"Everything's wrong. Young Chauncey and all the rest of the young people we've trained have walked out en bloc. I'll deal with them later. Right now we've got the passengers to think of and if we don't do something quickly they'll get restive. You have a full controlling staff down at the space grounds?"

"Yes—they're all there."

"Good. That means all the original instructors on space flight. A round dozen of them. The only way to save this situation is for you and the rest of the instructors to turn into pilots for this initial flight. We'll have to do without hostesses, unless you can contact the women who did the original training under the orders."

Sedberg ran a finger along his lips. "This is an awkward situation and no mistake. I don't know whether—"

"We've no time to argue about it, man: we've got to have action. The whole success of the Corporation depends on this initial take-off. It's another variation of "the show must go on!"

*   *   *

The door opened and shut as Sedberg went on his way. Manton gave a hard smile and whipped up the private phone connecting with his home.

"Get me my wife, Jackson," he said briefly, as the man servant responded. Then, a moment or so later: "That you, Ann? Where is Elise? She's on late turn at the Exchange, isn't she?"

"Yes. She's in bed at the moment. Do you want me to call her?"

"Tell her to get dressed and come to the space ground headquarters right away. I want to thrash something out with her."

"What is it, Randle?" There was sudden anxiety in Ann's voice, "I know that tone of yours. What's she been doing?"

"Far as I can see she's been concealing vital information from me—me, her own father! The Union of the Young has gone on strike, Ann—left me flat without a pilot or hostess. I'm having to do the best I can. Elise must have known about all this, but she never gave me a hint of warning."

"Perhaps she didn't know—"

"She knew, all right! Send her along, Ann."

Manton rang off before he could be involved in further argument.

For a moment he sat thinking, then he glanced up in surprise at a knock on the door.

"Come in," Manton said—and Meredith, the meteorologist, entered. He was not looking particularly happy, either.

"Hello, Meredith," Manton greeted. "You seem to have dropped out of my life recently. Have a seat."

"Thanks." The weatherman sat down and set his briefcase on the table. Then he sat as though trying to get his thoughts into order.

"This won't take long, will it?" Manton asked. "I have an important appointment coming up any moment, with my daughter."

"I'll make it as brief as I can," Meredith promised, coming back to life and unfastening his briefcase. "You delegated me to examine the possibility of climatic weather stations and I went out into space for just that purpose. I said at the board meetings that I'd let you have a full report when I'd worked it out—"

"Yes, yes. Come to the point, man. Are climatic stations a possibility or not? That'll all I need to know."

"Definitely not. I think you'd create no end of atmospheric trouble if you had the scientists try it. In any case, I think there will be trouble by natural causes in the long run. It's no use precipitating anything."

Manton took his cigar slowly out of his mouth. "Trouble? What kind of trouble?"

"The weather situation throughout the world has undergone an enormous change since the atomic war." Meredith said. "You will have noticed for yourself the absence of direct sunlight since the war ended."

"Uh-huh. I've noticed." For a moment there dritted across Manton's mind the memory of something Ann had said. Something about there being rainbows.

"In countries which normally expect sunlight all the year round there has been none since the war ended," Meredith continued, "I have checked up on that. The veil is over everywhere, from tropics to Arctic—and from outer space none of the Earth's surface can be seen for cloud.... High above the veil, at the limits of the atmosphere belt, there is a wide hand of thicker vapor, encircling Earth like a ring of Saturn. It is composed entirely of aqueous vapor and it is becoming slowly heavier."

Manton shrugged. "Well, it will dissipate, won't it? I'm not much of a scientist, but that seems the obvious conclusion. I recall that clouds of dust covering the Earth were once blown off by a volcanic eruption and gave amazing sunsets. But it dissipated in time."

"Mmmm—Krakatoa." Meredith nodded moodily. "I'm afraid there is no comparison between Krakatoa and what is happening now. You see, it has all happened before. There was a time, ages ago, when Earth had a similar vaporous ring. When the ring reached saturation point it collapsed. Or in the words of the Bible, the 'heavens opened'. It has become known as the Deluge."

"Oh, that!" Manton laughed shortly. "You don't believe that nonsense, surely—about Noah and his Ark, Arrarat, and all the rest of it?"

"Matter of fact I do, because there is strong scientific evidence to support it—the catastrophe anyway. It is in the records that a huge canopy of vapors covered the world of the pre-deluge man, much the same as the vapors which now embrace Jupiter and Saturn. In those days the vapors were caused by the boiling oceans evaporating from a young, hot world. In this modern age we have reproduced the ferment and heat with nuclear fission, which is giving the same effect."

Manton got to his feet. "But—this is fantastic! Surely there is some way of breaking it up?"

"We could break it up, but we'd simply precipitate the trouble, that's all. That vapor is water, Mr. Manton—untold multimillions of gallons of it, soaked up sea water and natural rain water. Break it up and it would be like pulling the bung out of a titanic barrel. It won't come down as rain, but as a solid, shattering deluge the like of which we can hardly imagine."

CHAPTER SIX

Manton had received a shock: there was no doubt of that, but after a moment or two he recovered himself and returned his cigar to his mouth.

"You're a disturbing devil, Meredith," he grinned.

"Sorry about that, sir, but you wanted the facts. I've got weather bureaus throughout the world checking my charts and up to now most meteorologists have agreed with me. From all of this it's plain why climatic stations wouldn't be much use. The whole face of things has changed since the war. Directions have altered. We'll have to recast a complete isobaric map of the world before we can even think about climatic control."

Manton shrugged. "Okay. Now we know where we are...." He looked at his cigar for a moment. "About this deluge idea? Can it happen in, say, our lifetime?"

"There'll be every warning in the drop in barometric pressure," Meredith said. "Even a look at your own at home will help to guide you. If you see a steady drop through the days which ends in 28 minus five—in other words, rock bottom—you can expect trouble."

"I'll remember," Manton said, and a troubled look crossed his face when the weatherman had departed. He was not given much opportunity to think about the matter, however for Sedberg came in urgently.

"I've managed it," he said. "Been some job, but with myself and those I've located we've got enough men togther to form a team of pilots. In regard to hostesses, our womenfolk are willing to do what they can along with the original tutors. They'll not be experts, but it's better than nothing."

"Good!" Manton adjusted himself to the change of subject. "How soon can you he ready?"

"About a couple of hours. Shall I convey that information to the passengers?"

Manton nodded. "Do that, and I'll be there personally at the take-off to explain what's happened."

Sedberg said no more. He quickly departed; and he had no sooner gone than Elise presented herself quietly dressed, as pretty as a picture. With unerring movements she advanced to the desk, stopping when she felt it touch her.

"I believe you want me, dad."

"Yes. I definitely do." Manton took her arm. "Sit down, my dear."

He settled her in the chair, looked at her reflectively, then crossed to his own side of the desk.

"I'll come straight to the point, Elise. There has been a walk-out of space pilots and hostesses, led by Nick Chauncey, head of the Union of the Young. I've managed to patch things up so that the spaceships will leave as arranged, though some time behind schedule. Now, why didn't you warn me that Chauncey was going to attempt something of this kind?"

Elise laughed slightly. "Because I am your daughter you don't tell me all your business secrets, do you? I'm a member of the Union of the Young, certainly, because I believe in its aims—but when I entered the Union I swore an oath to never reveal any of its plans. All members must do that. It was not a question of my doing you a disservice: it was a matter of loyalty."

"You—you believe in what they are fighting for? How can you? Set against your own father and the ideals for which he is fighting night and day. I ask you to resign from the Union."

"Ideals like yours, dad, have been cherished by industralists and commercial giants ever since civilization began. They always follow the same pattern of Grab. And they always end up by putting down what they have built up. That is what the Union is against, what every young person is against, and what I am against. I'm sorry to disobey you, but I will not leave."

"This matter is too serious for me to argue about it." Manton said curtly. "Either you cut free from the Union of the Young, or I shall have to disown you. You know what that means, and with your affliction you can't afford to risk it."

Elise got to her feet slowly. "Sometimes a decided move is necessary to prove one's faith in an ideal," she said quietly. "I believe in one thing, and you believe in another. I shall remain with the Union, no matter what."

Elise turned uncertainly and then found her way to the door. Manton was so astonished at the way things had gone he did not rise to help her. He only came to himself when the door had closed.

*   *   *

Elise kept her word. After her brief interview with her father she returned home, collected a few personal possessions into a suitcase, and then prepared to depart again. She only told her anxious mother that she could not agree with her father's outlook, and then she left.

She did her afternoon turn at the telephone exchange and then set about finding lodgement. As was always the case, she was helped by passers-by, and eventually found a city hotel well suited to her needs and pocket as a business girl. This done, she went direct to the Union of the Young headquarters, arriving just as Nick Chauncey was at the end of taking a meeting. Catching sight of her at the back of the room he finished speechifying and came down from the dais.

"You're late," he said anxiously. "I was beginning to fear that something had happened."

"Something has. That was what delayed me." Elise submitted to being led to a quiet corner and then continued: "I'm on my own, Nick."

"Your own?" He frowned a little: then as the girl explained the situation became clear.

"That is how much I believe in the Union, and in you," she finished. "I couldn't make it much clearer, could I?"

"Nobody on earth could have made it clearer." Nick embraced her tightly. "The Union apart, I'm glad you believe in me. All the same, I'm worried about you."

"Worried, dearest? Why should you be?"

"If I could ask you to marry me, I would," Nick went on, still holding her. "Believe that, Elise! Only I haven't got the money. All I have is what I saved during the training period as a pilot, and a bit before that from my normal job. At the moment I've no job at all. But I'll be finding one. My whole concentration is on the formation of the rival space line. I was just telling the gang about it when you came in."

"How far have you got? What's the set-up?"

"Pretty good at the moment, thanks to lots of the boys being busy while I was out in space. The financiers are ready to back the deal, and quite a few shadow factories up and down the country are waiting to go into action. It's all a matter of waiting for modified plans of the Sedberg spaceship to come from the designers—our own boys again, of course. They're hurrying all they can. Once that happens I see no reason why the Chauncey Corporation should not be formed. Unless..." and a shadow darkened Nick's vital young face.

"What?"

"So much depends on your father and what he'll do. After the walkout it's not likely that he'll let things rest at that. He'll smash up the union if he possibly can, and he's got power and money enough to do it, too."

"One thing will block him," Elise said. "I'm in the Union, and he knows it. Whatever happens to the rest will happen to me, and for all his faults I don't think dad will want to smash me."

And in that guess Elise was correct. Not that Randle Manton did not attempt to smash the Union of the Young: he did, by every means in his power short of actual violence. He tried every legal trick to have the Union disbanded, or declared illegal, but even his power was not sufficient to reverse the laws of the country.

So, as far as Nick Chauncey was concerned, he continued his activities unmolested. Modified plans of the Sedberg space machine were duly forthcoming and the actual building of the machines in the shadow factories began. They were not as luxurious as the ships Manton was using but mechanically they were absolutely dependable. As fast as they came off the production line they were transported to the great area, formerly a natural park, which the financiers had bought up as the future Chauncey space grounds.

One surprise which Manton had not reckoned with and which certainly affected his plans for the future, was the report that Venus was not an empty world, as the first expedition had reported. This fact became obvious when the first tourists returned to Earth around Christmas time and Sedberg took it upon himself to break the news.

"But how the devil did you come to miss it on the first occasion?" Manton demanded. "I thought you made a thorough investigation."

"We did." Sedberg shrugged. "That is, as thorough as one can be on a planet smothered in fog, mists, violent winds, and thunderstorms. Naturally, in the short time we were there we did not cover every mile of Venus' surface. However, to cut things short—there is a civilisation, about the only one so far as we know at present. It is on the southeast corner of the planet, spread over an enormous windswept planteau. The people are not unlike us—which isn't unusual with a world about the same size. The only thing is that they are revoltingly ugly by our standards."

"I gather you made contact with them, then?"

"Yes, I took the risk. They are quite an amicable people with a science and social grade about like our own. But they haven't got space travel. The language problem was a tough one but I managed to make myself understood somehow, and I left them a load of books and tapes on the English language so we can converse better next time."

Manton listened with no expression on his face. Then he asked a question.

"How did they react to the visit of Earth people?"

"Favorably, on the whole. As I say, they were friendly. We shall not be able to take any of the wealth of Venus without coming to an arrangement with Inva Krefel. That's the name of the ruler, or emperor, of the civilization. I found him polite but guarded. And as I have said, abominably ugly."

"Mmmm," Manton said, his brow lowering. "Next time you're on the Venus trip, Sedberg, find out what represents value to him. It may be only dirt to us and that way we're not out of pocket. If he wants something that represents value to us we'll try some other dodge. I certainly don't intend to try to bargain with him for precious metal and stones. We'd lose all the profit."

"All right, but I'm warning you. He isn't the kind of man to be trifled with, and their science is easily the equal of ours if it came to a test of arms."

"You don't think I'd go that far, do you? Anyway if they have not got space travel, the luck is all on our side."

About this time, too, the lunar expedition returned for fresh supplies—and with a truly amazing story of their findings. On the moon there was inconceivable wealth in the shape of gold and silver chiefly, and a limited amount of uranium. Except for the cost of the mining expedition it was more or less sheer profit all along the way. With such a glittering prize Manton could hardly be blamed for forgetting that he had promised not to become over-ambitious.

So absorbed did he become he forgot all about the Union of the Young—but the Union of the Young did not forget him, a fact which became apparent in the spring when notices appeared overnight on boardings and in the press—radio and television being barred because Manton controlled them—advertising the Chauncey Space Line, together with the fare prices. This advent hit Manton with the force of a bomb, particularly the prices, which were way below his own.

"Just a flash in the pan," he told Ann that evening. "I've been expecting something like it, but I never seemed able to lay my hands on the Union. It won't last."

Nick Chauncey's line continued without interference. In the beginning he did most of the piloting himself, together with those who had been trained in the Manton Corporation, and there was certainly no lack of hostesses—so the line progressed. And Nick always took care that no approach was made to areas which Manton had staked out. In fact, on each visit to Mars and Venus, Nick arranged to have as many flags as possible, in his own company's name, duly staked, with the result that he rapidly gained more staked-out territory than Manton himself.

Spring, summer, and fall Nick was hard at it. In the fall he ceased to be a pilot and moved over to the executive side instead. Elise was there, too, mainly as telephonist to the company, but also doing a good deal of work that did not demand sight for its execution.

For a time, Manton toyed with the idea of coming to some kind of compromise with Nick Chauncey. Then a new thought struck him. The small Chauncey machines which were getting all the inner planet business were not made to withstand the rigors of extra long journeys—to the giant major planets of Jupiter, Saturn, Uranus and Neptune. When he discovered this fact, Manton smiled broadly and immediately advertised the fact that his line was willing to undertake the trips—exclusively.

Then, indeed, catastrophe struck him. Four of his tours were lost one after the other. From what few details were known, the first crashed on Jupiter, due to its enorrnous gravity against which inexperienced pilots were helpless. The remaining three crashed while attempting variously to land on Saturn, Uranus and Neptune. After these incidents, and the court of inquiry which Manton had to face—and from which a skilled lawyer pulled him out safely by the skin of his teeth—Manton found his space line severely boycotted. Even had he made the move of reducing his prices to be on a level with Chauncey's, it would have done no good. He had lost the good-will of the public, and nothing could atone for that.

At which point Nick Chauncey came personally into the picture again—right into Manton's city office one morning, as a matter of fact.

"You're got your nerve," Manton said coldly, motioning to a chair. "What the devil do you want here, Chauncey?"

"Do I need to tell you?" Nick's face was unsmiling. "I've come to buy your space line."

"And what makes you think I want to sell it?"

"The fact you're businessman enough not to run anything at a loss."

"Just a few reverses don't make any difference to me, Chauncey. The line stays as it is, out of your reach. Besides, I'm using part of it for freightage—ores and so forth."

"Why not say the minerals and precious stones your well-paid pirates have stolen from Venus, and have done with it?"

"Get out!" Manton said coldly. "And if you come here again you'll be sorry!"

Nick waited a second or two, then with a shrug he got to his feet.

"Okay, if that's how you want it—but remember what I've said. You know my address if you want me.... the Chauncey Space Line. I'll always be ready to talk business."

Nick went on his way, not altogether surprised with the result of his interview. Once he reached his headquarters he told an anxiously waiting Elise how things had gone.

"I've simply played a hunch," he confessed when he had finished. "You once said the space line would fall into my hands like a ripe plum. This seemed to be the moment when it would happen, but evidently I guessed wrong."

Elise shook her head slowly, gazing into distance in that strange way she had.

"No, you didn't guess wrong. Nick. You acted a trifle prematurely perhaps, but in the end it will come about—because it has to."

CHAPTER SEVEN

Elise was right. Two months later Manton's hand was forced. Nobody was any longer interested in his space line, after the debacle of the outer planets. Even a fool could see that Nick Chauncey had got all the business. So, at an extraordinary meeting of the directors, Manton got the necessary authority to sell out, at the same time retaining just a few machines with which he could still operate the mining side of his business.

The price paid for the defunct line was, in Manton's view, scandalously low. In Chauncey's view, it was exorbitantly high. But at the end of the wrangling Chauncey finally got his way and thereby became the managing director of the only space line in the world.

*   *   *

Following the transference of the space line to Chauncey there seemed to come a time when nothing of vital interest occurred. In general, as far as Nick was concerned anyway, it was a period of intensive effort, with him straining every nerve and sinew to make his space line a success. And indeed it was.

There was one point which Nick did not see in his urgent struggles, or if he did see it, it did not dawn upon him that it constituted danger—and that was that certain Venusians came to Earth, on a sort of reciprocal welcome system. No harm in that, certainly. But among them was Inva Krefel, the recognized ruler of Venus, now in possession of the English language thanks to the books and tapes which had been left for him. And the first person he visited was Randle Manton.

It was Manton's first contact with a man of another world, and he was not at all sure that he liked it. The ugliness of Inva Krefel was phenomenal, judged by Earth standards. He had a dull gray face, bulbous nose, and tiny little eyes buried in rims of puffy flesh. His mouth, which never smiled, was thickly sensuous and to add to the generally revolting effect, he was utterly bald—a feature which he had in common with all the males of his race. Apart from that he was a magnificently built man, standing a good seven or eight inches over six feet, and massively muscled. But there was around him a strange aura, an utterly alien quality, which all his civilized clothing and impeccable manners could not dissipate.

"This," Manton said uncertainly, "is a most unexpected honor, Inva Krefel."

"A surprise, too, I imagine." the Venusian said, in his curiously liquid bass. "Since your space line has so often sent tourists to my humble planet, I thought I would return the compliment."

"Of course—of course. Er—won't you be seated, Excellency?"

The dough-faced giant complied and sat with the stiffness of a totem pole, his tiny eyes watching Manton's every move. He for his part settled at the opposite side of his desk, his whole manner one of intense wariness. Normal people he could deal with instantly, but this was something new.

"You have a pleasant planet, though it is a little too chilly for my liking," the Venusian resumed presently. "However, I did not come to discuss your climate, but to deal with business... What is the reason for denuding several of the mountains of my world of carbon?"

"Carbon?" Manton repeated politely, his mind racing.

"Certain explorers have taken large quantities of carbon, in a condition known as diamonds on your world, and have transported them back to Earth. No permission was asked for. It was pure theft. Why," Krefel asked deliberately, "did it happen?"

"Do you mean that some of the spaceship crews have dared to thieve on your territory, Excellency?"

"Deliberately and repeatedly. Ever since the first visit to our world when I extended hospitality."

Manton could see the danger lights quite clearly and did his best to steer around them.

"I am shocked and surprised to hear of such vandalism, Excellency," he said slowly. "As it happens, I cannot accept the responsibility because the space line is no longer my concern. I sold it to a—a younger man a few months ago. I have so many other interests I could no longer deal with it."

"I am aware that the space line now runs under the auspices of the Chauncey Space Line, but the machines which were engaged on these thefts had your insignia upon them. Can you account for that?"

"I can only suggest that Chauncey—or some of the men working for him—are attempting theft and piracy. It's still not a concern of mine. You should deal with Chauncey himself."

"I will do so," the Venusian decided. "If I cannot get satisfaction from him I will return here." He rose to his gigantic height. "I must remark, Mr. Manton, that I take a very grave view of this business. Permission to visit our world and, maybe, establish the basis of trading, hardly included outright thieving."

And while Manton thought out what he must do next, the putty-faced giant of Venus, accompanied by two equally gigantic members of his entourage, crossed the city and finished up at the executive headquarters of the Chauncey Space Line. After a good deal of preliminary haggling Inva Krefel ultimately found himself in a big private office with only Elise Manton present. Her nimble fingers were quickly sorting card indices into a drawer, but she paused as she sensed the giant's nearness.

"Something I can do for you?" she inquired, and Krefel wondered vaguely why she seemed to look right through him.

"I am seeking Mr. Nicholas Chauncey, and I was informed I would find him here."

Elise hesitated and frowned. She had never heard a voice like this before—mellow, soothing, and deeply bass. In her mind's eye she saw something quite beautifully masculine.

"I'm afraid Mr. Chauncey is away for a few days, but I am his confidential secretary, if there is any message you would care to leave."

"I think not. My business is exclusively with him." The Venusian was still staring with his little eyes. "Forgive me asking the question, but is it the custom of Earth women to look right through a visitor? I am not experienced with them since I am of another world."

"Another world?" Elise repeated blankly.

"I am Inva Krefel of Venus. At least you Earth people call it Venus."

"The—the ruler of the planet?" Elise ejaculated.

"That is so."

"Oh, do forgive me. I hadn't realized—do sit down."

She felt quickly for her own chair and seated herself. Inva Krefel sat down also and still looked at her.

"I am grateful for one thing," he said. "As I remarked, I have had little experience of Earth women, and those I have seen have instantly shied away from me. Why, I do not know... You do not do that."

"No," Elise agreed. "I cannot think of any reason why I should."

"I am complimented." The Venusian mused for a moment. "Might I inqure your name?"

"Elise Manton."

Krefel's eyebrows rose. "Are you in some way related to Randle Manton?"

"Indeed, yes. His daughter."

"How very interesting."

"My father and I are on opposite sides of the fence, so to speak," Elise said quietly. "I belong to another school of thought entirely—a young school of thought. So I work alongside Nick Chauncey and help him in every way I can."

"I understand. This is a personal question, so forgive it. Are you married to him?"

"No. There are reasons."

"I cannot imagine what they can be, unless, of course, that is because my knowledge of Earth customs is necessarily limited. You are young, attractive, and if I may so, quite beautiful."

Elise laughed a trifle embarrassedly. "You're very flattering, Excellency."

"Not at all: I state fact, as I always do."

"I'm sorry Mr. Chauncey isn't her," Elise said, picking up the conversation again.

"No matter, Miss Manton. I am staying on Earth for a few days and I will call again. Perhaps he'll have returned by Friday?"

"I should think it quite possible. In any case, I'll make an appointment for that day."

"Splendid." Krefel rose to his feet. and then hesitated for a moment. "I wonder if I might ask you a favor, Miss Manton?"

"But of course." Elise, realizing from the change of direction in the voice that Krefel now on his feet, rose also. "If I can help in any way..."

"You certainly can. Because of my high position I am not able to mix with the ordinary people of Earth and find out about their ways and customs, which I am most anxious to do. Would it be possible for you to spend an evening with me and explain a lot of things which are mystifying me?"

Elise did not answer immediately. Then Krefel added:

"I realize there will be difficulties for you, Miss Manton. I think you do exceedingly well to handle things as you do. I refer to your blindness, naturally."

"I'd rather hoped you would not notice it."

"Believe me, I probably would not have done so, only I am extra observant, being on a strange world amid strange people.... I can assure you of every courtesy if you will oblige me. My entourage will be always mindful of your comfort."

"Then—then I'll be glad to." Elise was rather breathless as she reflected that the chance to spend an evening with the ruler of a planet does not happen except in dreams—as a rule. "What am I to do? What time do you wish to see me?"

"My ADC—as I believe you Earth people call such a person—will present himself at your home or apartment at 7 o'clock this evening, and will drive you to my hotel. To make you entirely comfortable we will discuss in the lounge, where you will be surrounded by people of your own planet. That will, perhaps, give you a feeling of complete security."

"Yes, I'll be ready," Elise promised, her last doubts vanishing. "I have an apartment in the Main Street Block, No. 11. I'll be waiting at 7 o'clock."

"Splendid." Krefel's unsmiling face surveyed her young figure and the eagerness of her face.

*   *   *

Some six hours after the visitation of Inva Krefel Randle Manton had another visitor. He was not feeling particularly in the mood to see anybody, but the man's visiting card sounded impressive—Dr. Henry Welton, Ph.D., so perhaps he was worth five minutes. When he was shown into the office he turned out to be a stoop-shouldered man of late middle-age, thin-faced and gray-haired, but with eyes alight with keenness.

"I am one of the few scientists left from the Atomic War, Mr. Manton," Welton said. "I won't beat about the bush. I am a very poor man—not through any fault of my own but because I have spent everything I own in private scientific research. Now I'm nearly at rock-bottom and I need a man such as you to save me."

Manton turned and smiled coldly. "Aren't you in the wrong office, doctor? I am not a moneylender."

"Mmm—I appreciate that. But you are a financier, and a man who handles millions. A man, shall I say, interested in yet another way to make millions?"

"Another way?" Manton was a trifle more interested.

"Let's face it, Mr. Manton. Everybody knows you took a severe beating from Nicholas Chauncey when he took over your space line. You must have lost heavily, and judging from the profits which he is now making, you are still losing. You would like something to replace the space line, and I would like to get some ready cash. So perhaps we can come to some arrangement?"

"About what? Come to the point, man!"

"The absolute certain cure for carcinoma—or more vulgarly, cancer."

Manton stared for a moment, then a slow smile of disbelief crossed his face.

"I have heard such claims before, doctor."

"I came with two women and one man, all of whom were given up for lost by the medical profession. They have medical certificates stating that they are now perfect with no trace of cancer whatever. Do you wish to see them? They're in the reception office."

"How do I know they're genuine?"

"You can contact the hospitals in which they were patients, and ask any question you like of the doctors concerned."

Manton was accustomed to smelling rats, but on this occasion he failed to do so. For a moment or two he pondered, and then switched on the intercom.

"Yes, Mr. Manton."

"There are two women and a man in the reception office. Send them in to me right away."

"Very good, sir."

Manton switched off again and stood waiting. In the meantime, Dr. Welton gave a tired smile and surveyed the gloomy gray scene outside the big window. Then the door clicked and Manton reflected that he had never seen three healthier-looking people than those who now entered his office. In every way they radiated strength and a general impression of buoyancy.

"I will not take up much of your time," Manton said briefly. "I understand each one of you has been cured of cancer?"

"In the last stages," the man confirmed. "All thanks to Dr. Welton here and his machine."

"You were in hospital before that? Which hospital?" Manton poised over his scratch pad, pencil ready.

"Main City—each one of us."

"Under which doctor?"

"Dr. Lawson, the cancer specialist."

"And your names?"

The man gave his name first and the women last. Then Manton straightened again.

"Thank you. That's all I wanted to know."

The three nodded and departed. Manton considered for a moment.

"On the face of it, doctor, I'm prepared to take a gamble," he said finally, "but I'll not do anything definite until I have contacted the hospital doctor. In the meantime, what do you suggest?"

"I suggest that I leave these." Welton raised his briefcase, opened it, and brought out some blue prints and specifications. "Here are the designs of large-sized machines, by which one could cure en masse. In the specifications are the full details of how to do it, and the formula for the radiations I incorporate."

"You have a radiation basis, then? Same as x-rays are normally used for carcinoma sufferers?"

"Precisely so. In this case I use entronium, which when treated in the manner described, is forced to release its energy. This in turn is 'tamed' to produce the necessary radiations through specially designed projectors."

"Entronium, eh?" There was a grim shadow on Manton's face. "How did you get hold of that?"

"As a scientist I look in all sorts of places—just as a bookworm infests all the second-hand stores I got the entronium at the Interplan Exchange, where, as you know, many of the precious gems, residue metals, and isotopes are sold at low prices. Chiefly stuff from other worlds."

"I see. Then I'll make you a proposition, doctor. If you are prepared to leave these specifications and designs with me, for my scientific staff to study, I will give you 1,000 credits as receipt. And, of course, a written receipt as well."

"Very well," Welton said, with his tired smile. "The invention is protected by patent in my name so, until we come to an arrangement, it is legally mine. You will forgive the safeguards?"

Manton nodded. "I'd forgive it. I'd think you a fool if you did not protect your interests.... But tell me, why did you come to me? Why not the hospital authorities?"

"Because, Mr. Manton, I have sweated blood and as good as wrecked my health to perfect this invention. The authorities controlling the hospitals might well think that I ought to give the invention for the sheer joy of helping suffering humanity. While I want to help I also have to live. So I came to the man with commercial insight."

"Sound policy," Manton said, pulling his cheque book out of a drawer and scribbling vigorously. "Here you are, Dr. Welton, and here—" He scribbled an official receipt, "here is our acknowledgement of the stuff you are leaving behind... Now where do I get in touch with you after my scientists have been busy?"

"The Elms, Dorsay St. I have one of these old-world, prewar houses where I can work without interruption. No telephone."

"Okay." Manton scribbled it down. "And I'll be in touch with you soon enough, doctor."

Satisfied, the old scientist left the office. Manton did not waste any time. He summoned the head of his scientific staff immediately and turned the papers and formula over to him, with orders for an early report. Then he set himself to think.

"Entronium," he muttered. "Davis was the man responsible for getting that, and now he's over at Chauncey's place. Wonder how the land lies? If Inva Krefel has had anything to say yet?"

It was not Manton's way to wonder about anything, so he picked up the phone and dialled the executive headquarters of the Chauncey Line. He was distinctly surprised when Elise answered him, after the usual reception telephonist.

"Hello, dad." Her voice had an unusually excited quality. "Something wrong?"

"I simply want to speak to Chauncey. Is he there?"

"Not until Friday. Sorry. Any message?"

"No. You might be able to help. I want to contact one of my former space pilots who is now working for Chauncey. Probably he's away on a run...Davis. Bob Davis."

"I'll find out. Just a minute." There was a long pause, then Elise's voice resumed. "As it happens, he's doing some maintenance between flights and I can get him for you. On the phone, do you mean?"

"No, no—at my office. As soon as possible, I must see him."

"All right, Dad, I'll tell him. Good-bye."

CHAPTER EIGHT

Within an hour, Davis presented himself. He seemed uncertain of himself, not at all sure whether he was on the carpet or not. However, Manton's manner was affable enough.

"Take a seat, Davis. Something important has come up. Sure you could spare the time to come and see me?"

"Yes. It's okay, Mr. Manton. Chauncey is away at the moment."

"So I believe. I'll come straight to the point. There are two items you should know about—one is that Inva Krefel, the big man on Venus, is aware of your pilfering and so forth on his planet and was in here this morning prepared to make trouble. I shifted the blame to Chauncey and he can wriggle out of it as best he can. If you're implicated, you'll get no help from me. I told you at the first that, though I'd reward you handsomely, I'd take no responsibility. Right?"

"Right," Davis nodded. "That was quite understood. So you want me and the boys to lie low on 'pilfering' for the time being. Is that it?"

"It would have been, but something else has turned up—which comprises the second item....Why did entronium get as far as the Interplan Exchange?"

Davis shrugged. "Entronium is a waste product, and you gave me permission to sell all waste products where I could, and collect the profits. You told me you were only interested in the really valuable stuff—diamonds, uranium—when we can get it—and so forth. Entronium is no good to anybody as far as big money is concerned. I collected a bit for it—not much. And the Interplan Exchange won't get much if they happen to sell it."

"They already have sold it, for a good figure. However, I'm not going into that, nor am I blaming you for selling the entronium. But here's the essential thing—I must get more entronium, as much of it as possible and as quickly as possible. What can you do about it?"

Davis thought for a moment. "I can get it easily enough—bags of it, but things are different now the Venusian big-shot has got onto the trick. It's going to make it tough."

"I realize that, but you'll have to chance it. You should have a good opportunity at present while Inva Krefel is spending his time on Earth here. When are you next due to make a run to Venus?"

"In two days."

"Good enough. This time the vessel will have the Chauncey insignia on it, which is all to the good. If there's any trouble, he'll be the one to receive it. Up to now you've made sneak visits in one of my own vessels, during your Earth 'liberty time', but that's out from now on. Krefel knows too much."

Davis nodded and got to his feet. "All right, Mr. Manton, I'll do my best.... Incidentally, how about something extra for danger money?"

"I'll see you're all right."

*   *   *

So Manton set in motion the wheels of what he hoped would be a major industry and, for the time being, events moved into their normal perspective. On the Friday Nick Chauncey returned from his business trip he found an efficient, but somehow different Elise awaiting him.

"Anything fresh?" he asked, after giving the girl his usual warm embrace.

"Just one thing—Inva Krefel, the ruler of Venus, wants to see you."

Nick turned to the intercom and switched it on. "Okay. Ask his Excellency to come in."

He stood waiting, and in another moment or two the enormous Venusian quietly entered while a clerk shut the door behind him. Nick advanced, trying to disguise the revulsion he felt at the man's atrocious ugliness.

"Good morning, Excellency." He motioned to a chair. "I haven't had the honor of meeting you before, though I've seen many members of your race.... Oh, this is my secretary, Miss Manton."

"I have already had the pleasure," the Venusian murmured, seating himself; then with a slight change of tone, "And now to business, Mr. Chauncey."

"Certainly. What can I do for you?"

"I'll tell you. You can stop your pilots stealing valuable gems and carbon, to say nothing of other things, from my planet. It's a lucrative game for you, Mr. Chauncey, I don't doubt—but the time has come to put a stop to it."

Nick colored hotly, then he remembered the high status of his visitor and somehow controlled himself.

"I was not aware that any thieving has been going on. Naturally I'll look into it right away."

"That is the least you can do."

Nick thought for a moment. "You are quite sure that it is my line which is responsible?"

"Of course. On the last four occasions thieves have been seen at work, using machines with the Manton spaceline insignia on them."

"Manton!" Nick ejaculated. "Then why implicate me?"

"Because I am satisfied that you are responsible, mainly because the thefts have occurred since you took full control. The use of Manton machines I merely regard as a cover-up. Naturally you have quite a few Manton machines in your fleet."

"Then what are you going to do?" Nick demanded, his face grim. "Obviously you think me guilty—which is entirely wrong—and you will exact recompense."

"Of course, but in the quietest possible way. After studying the situation I have come to the conclusion that a controller like you is not fit to have charge of space machines. It demands an older and, need I add, a more honorable man. Therefore, I have decided to back Randle Manton to the limit with money and concessions in the re-establishtnent of his former space line, and to withdraw from you all permission to land, or circle near, my planet."

"At least give me time to prove that you are wrong about me!" Nick insisted. "You owe me that much. I'll get to the bottom of this thieving if it takes me the rest of my life."

Krefel shrugged. "I will listen to whatever evidence you produce, but my orders stand just the same. Good morning, Mr. Chauncey."

Without a handshake or glance back over his shoulder the Venusian strode out of the office and closed the door. Very slowly Nick turned until he was facing Elise. She was gazing into space, but the general hunch of her shoulders seemed to indicate how dispirited she felt.

"Any comments?" Nick asked her, starting to prowl.

"How can I have? You can't fight a man as powerful as Krefel. With him and dad working together you're as good as sunk, Nick."

"Well, thanks for the pep talk." Nick rubbed the back of his neck fiercely. "There must be some way around this."

"I don't think there is. I've some idea of how determined Krefel is about this whole thing. He's hinted at it quite a lot in the few times I've seen him."

Nick turned. "Seen him? You mean—"

"I mean I've been out with him a few times while you have been away. When he learned I was Elise Manton he seemed to want to know me better, and— All that apart, he's a charming companion, and his manners are far above those of many Earth men I know."

"You're forcing me to be blunt, but I'll have to do it," Nick said quietly. "Krefel's only interest in you must be because he has some idea of making use of you because you're Manton's daughter. He couldn't be interested in you as a woman. You know why, as well as I do. And besides, you're Earthian and he's Venusian. These can't be any physical attraction."

"If you think because I'm blind he isn't interested you're vastly mistaken. I know he is by the things he's said."

"Such as?" Nick snapped, already irritated beyond measure with the things which had happened to him

"I don't intend to repeat his remarks. They were personal." Elise was coldly silent for a moment or two, then: "And there's no reason why a Venusian shouldn't be interested in an Earthian. Whites marry blacks. don't they, on Earth here? Why shouldn't it operate between planets?"

"You're moving fast, Elise, aren't you? Who said anything about marrying?"

"I'm merely giving you an example—or hasn't it dawned on you that with space travel the day is bound to come when interplanetary marriages will be the accepted thing?"

"It dawned on me long ago, but this hardly seems the place or the time to discuss it. In any case, there won't be many interplanetary romances if all the Venusians measure up to Krefel for ugliness."

"Ugliness..." Elise repeated slowly.

"That's what I said. Not just ordinary ugliness, either, such as you find in a human being, but something downright revolting."

Elise laughed a little to herself. "Perhaps there is some compensation in not being able to see him, then. From his voice I pictured somebody altogether magnificent."

"So that's what's leading you astray, is it? The voice? I'll grant it's a mellow one, but it doesn't match the man." Nick moved impulsively and gripped Elise by the shoulders. "Look, Elise, I'm sorry if I've said something I shouldn't, but it has come as a bit of a shock to find you so enraptured with this Venusian. Right on top of smashing my space line, too." Elise drew herself away and with unerring instinct drifted toward the window. After a moment or two she spoke.

"What do you think has really happened regarding these thefts from Venus?"

"Perfectly obvious—your father's responsible. I allowed him to retain one or two machines so he could continue his lunar mining. One or two machines have evidently stepped out of line and gone to Venus, for the sole purpose of lifting what doesn't belong to them."

Elise turned in sudden anger. "Do you think for one moment that father would do a thing like that?"

"I'm perfectly sure he would! Not to get me in a mess, because he probably didn't think it would rebound on me anyhow—but to enrich himself. To do that, your father would set fire to the tail of the devil himself if need be."

"So that's what you really think about him!"

"Certainly—and so do you, if you spoke the truth. This is Manton's World, isn't it? If it isn't altogether, it soon will be."

Elise turned, and after a few hesitating movements took her hat from the big stand by the window. Tight-lipped she settled it firmly on her fair hair.

"Where are you going?" Nick asked in surprise.

"I'm not sure at the moment, but certainly away from here. Since you've been away on business, Nick, you've changed incredibly."

Nick was so completely astounded he did not know what to say. He watched the girl's fingers feel sensitively for the doorknob, then in another moment she had gone. He was left staring at the panels.

*   *   *

Randle Manton was quite the most surprised man in the city when Inva Krefel called upon him and told him of his intentions. He was even more surprised when he learned of the ugly Venusian's interest in Elise—but, of course, because it suited his purpose he was a willing co-operator in whatever the Venusian wished.

At the end of an hour, after Krefel had gone Manton was aware of one thing. His space line was restored to him, greater than ever before, with unlimited Venusian wealth at the back of it. Manton was convinced now, that with the personal fortune he also intended to rake in from the cancer-destroying machines he could become one of the most powerful men on Earth—if not the most powerful. The destruction of Nick Chauncey and his pathetic Union of the Young was a certainty.

And it was at this point that Manton began thinking about Elise, and the Venusian's declarations that he was "interested" in her—which in such a high personage as Krefel was equivalent to saying that he was in love. What to do about Elise and how to prise her away from Nick Chauncey? Manton was debating this aspect when the girl herself came into his office. In every possible direction the gods seemed to be smiling.

"Elise! By all that's wonderful!" Manton got up from his desk and hurried across to embrace her.

"Hello, Dad. I didn't announce myself. I knew you wouldn't mind my walking in. The secretary told me you weren't in conference or anything."

"Even if I had been I wouldn't have missed this.... Here, have a seat."

Manton piloted the girl to a chair and then stood looking down on her, his craggy face smiling in genuine pleasure.

"You make up for the sunshine we don't get any more," he said at last. "Only one thing's bothering me: How soon are you going to slip off again?"

"I'm not going to. That's up to you. What chance have I of a job in your organization?"

The smile slowly left Manton's face. "Are you serious?"

"Never more serious in my life."

"But why the sudden change of course, my dear? I thought you were well and truly behind Nick Chauncey."

"I was, until I realized he had violated the very principles he is supposed to be fighting. He has sworn war against ambition for ambition's sake, yet now he's secretly thieving from Venus and pushing the blame on to you. Whatever I may think of your mistaken ideas, dad, it seems to me that Nick has let himself get out of hand in his bid for power."

"I see." Manton was glad at that moment that his daughter was unable to judge the expression on his face. "That sort of makes a difference, doesn't it? Are you aware that Inva Krefel has decided to restore the space line to me?"

"I am aware of it, yes."

"But I thought you were against my ambitions, as you call them?"

"There are a lot of things I don't agree with, but the way Nick Chauncey has turned out, he's even worse. Somehow, I don't really care any more about that. I'm coming where I'm wanted."

"Good girl! You're always wanted as far as I'm concerned."

"I know that, but there is somebody else, too."

Manton looked surprised. "Somebody else?"

"I'm talking about Inva Krefel. Hasn't he hinted at anything, between him and me?"

"He's mentioned that he is very interested in you, but I thought he was merely being polite."

"It's more than that," Elise said quietly. "Much more."

Manton put a hand gently on her shoulder. For the moment he could think of nothing more to say.

CHAPTER NINE

Through the ensuing days Nick Chauncey smouldered to himself. He considered himself—quite justifiably—a much-wronged man, and he refused to he consoled. He was waiting for only one thing—the return of his fleet from Venus. Then he could proceed to ferret out the truth concerning the Venusian thefts. Once he had that truth he could confront Krefel with it. The Venusian was still on Earth, showing no inclination to return home—and that was probably because Elise was the centre of his thoughts.

The arrival of the space fleet swung Nick into vigorous action. He waited only until all tourists had been disembarked—then, in company with several of his officials, he commenced a detailed search of each machine which had made the trip. Inevitably he came to the machine which Davis had piloted, and in the natural sequence of events he also came to one of the storage holds, lead-lined to prevent radioactive seepage. The hold was filled to the roof with entronium.

That was enough for Nick. He turned to the men with him as he tugged off the helmet of his insulated suit.

"Mount a guard over this," he ordered curtly. "I fancy Davis is going to answer a few questions."

In 10 minutes Davis was in the office, already expecting what was going to happen. He had realized it was practically inevitable that the entronium would be found when he had heard of the decision to conduct a thorough search of each machine. Now he cast around in his mind for excuses. And Chauncey came straight to the point.

"The safety hold of the F-20 is filled to the limit with radioactive entronium, Davis. What's the answer?"

Davis remained sullenly silent, shying away from the accusing glint in Nick's eyes.

"I know all about it." Nick went on bitterly. "Not only this theft, but plenty of others before it. All at the orders of Randle Manton. What's the explanation for this business?"

Davis shrugged. "Manton ordered me to get entronium, and that's what I did."

"You know the penalty for this?"

"I knew the risk, so since I've failed to make it, I'll have to accept my punishment. All I was trying to do was make extra money."

"Exactly, and your endeavours to make extra money have smashed my space line in bits. Krefel, the ruler of Venus, knows exactly what you're up to—and he'll certainly know about this particular theft of entronium, I don't doubt. I have been blamed for it all. But you're going to explain how it happened, and who gave you your orders. When you've done that, you'll get the punishment you deserve."

"But that means 10 to 15 years in jail!"

"You knew that when you started. Now come on..." Nick strode to the door. "We're both going this minute to see Manton. He can get Krefel to his office and hear the truth."

Davis, white-faced, hesitated—then he turned slowly as Nick stood waiting. Half way to the door Davis suddenly seemed to make up his mind about something. His hand darted into his uniform pocket and up to his mouth. He stopped walking and smiled crookedly.

"Won't be much use my coming, Chauncey," he said. "I had one more move left...and I've made it."

On the last word he reeled dizzily and crashed inert to the floor. It all happened so rapidly Nick had not the time to grasp things. The moment he did so he dashed across to the fallen pilot and examined him quickly. Then he strode to his desk and switched on the intercom.

"Get a doctor," he ordered curtly. "And quickly! There's a pilot here on the verge of death."

But despite the rapid arrival of the doctor and the breakneck drive to the hospital it was useless. Davis died on the way as the lethal pill he had swallowed had full effect. Nick came back to his office in a mood of dazed anger, bitterly aware of the fact that the one man who could tell the truth about the Venusian thefts was out of the picture forever.

During lunch his thoughts darted off on a new tack. Diamonds and precious stones he could well understand Manton trying to get

—but what in heaven's name could he want with entronium? A waste radioactive substance? There was nothing to he gained by asking him, of course, but Nick certainly wondered what kind of deal he had crippled by holding up the entronium.

Because he could not find the answer, Nick was obliged to shelve the problem for the time being and turn to immediate matters. He had the entronium unloaded from the spaceship and placed in a sealed vault in the executive building, heavily sheathed so there could be no harm done. Then he called a meeting of the Chauncey Company and laid the facts before them. What was to be done?

At first it was financiers who made the biggest fuss—until Nick Chauncey's own friends in the Union of the Young made it entirely clear how he had been victimized. After that the financiers took a slightly more lenient view. On one thing they were determined: they would remain in the company because they were fighting Manton, which was good and sufficient reason.

"We can still run tourists to Mars," Nick said finally: "There is nothing against that—and if we do it with proper precautions we can also run to the outer planets. Manton made a mess of it but we won't. I suggest we try it, if only to keep a line running in opposition to Manton."

After a good deal of argument his motion was carried. The outer planets would henceforth be included... But in that Nick had overlooked the type of man he was trying to defeat. Randle Manton did not like half-way measures. All or nothing was his policy, and therein lay the seeds of trouble for Nick Chauncey and, incidentally, the ideals of the Union of the Young.

*   *   *

Randle Manton knew exactly when the Chauncey fleet had returned from Venus, and therefore he became increasingly surprised when there was no word or sign from Davis. And Inva Krefel, in a brief visit in which he had told of the legal boycott of all Chauncey machines from Venus, had not mentioned the business of the entronium—so here again Manton was in the dark, and becoming increasingly worried. The completed full-size cancer-destroying machine had been ready for some days and only waited for the entronium. But where was Davis?

Added to this, Manton was also uneasy because he had already tentatively announced to the press, as well as on his own television and radio circuits, that he was on the verge of manufacturing machines to destroy cancer. If there was now to be a last minute hitch he would look a fool, which was hardly in keeping with his dominant, ever-growing influence.

That same evening, as he still waited for Davis, Manton got the answer to the riddle. At home, in the lounge, in the newspaper. A small paragraph reported the death of one Capt. Davis of the Chauncey Line, from "space strain". And that was all.

"I don't believe it," Manton muttered. "More likely something went wrong and he put himself out."

"Who did, dear?" Ann asked, glancing up from her novel.

"Nothing," Manton grunted, getting up from the armchair. "Just talking to myself. One of my deals seems to have sideslipped."

Ann smiled faintly. "Does that matter so much? Why must you always be dealing in something, Randle? You've got the space line back, thanks to His Excellency. And we've Elise back, too. What more do you want?"

"Oh, don't be ridiculous!" Manton snorted, biting the end off a cigar and lighting it viciously.

"Honestly," Ann went on, looking at him again, "I do wonder at times where things are going to end. Instead of being satisfied with what you have and the millions that go with it, you have— among other things—to bring that abominable Venusian into our home circle. I don't think I can be nice to him much longer, Randle."

"If it is in the interests of the Mantons you'll have to, Ann. You're part of the family, and I'm the head of that family. Let that be understood."

Manton did not give his wife the chance to answer. He strode from the room, en route for the library where he could give the Davis problem considered thought. As he passed through the hall his eye happened to settle on the big barometer against the wall. Diverted in thought for a moment he tapped the glass and watched the needle move down two degrees to exactly 30. Manton frowned, an almost forgotten interview with Meredith, the meteorologist, coming back into his mind.

"What did he say now?" Manton mused, chewing his cigar. "If there's a steady drop to minus 28 through a period of days you can expect trouble...."

He considered this through an interval and then laughed shortly to himself.

"Trouble!" he ejaculated. "As if I haven't got trouble enough without that...."

"I beg pardon, sir?"

Manton started as he noticed the manservant coming across from the kitchen regions.

"Nothing, Jackson. Just thinking out loud."

"Oh. I beg your pardon, sir. I was just coming to tell you that Miss Elise rang up a short while ago to say that she will be very late home. She's dining with His Excellency tonight at his hotel."

"Oh? Well, thanks, Jackson.... And why the delay in telling me?"

"I'm very sorry, sir. I'm afraid we domestics got interested in a television program in the kitchen."

"On one of my channels?" Manton grinned.

"No, sir—independent. A Mr. Meredith of the Central Weather Bureau was giving a talk about a circle of water surrounding the Earth. Very absorbing. It would almost seem as though every living soul of us is under a Sword of Damocles."

Manton did not say anything. He just stared with the most extraordinary expression on his tace. Then without another word he headed toward his study.

CHAPTER TEN

About this same time Nick Chauncey was addressing a capacity meeting of the Union of the Young in their greatly increased headquarters in the city centre. And Nick was no longer despondent or bitter. He looked like a man who has found the solution to all his problems—which in a sense he had. One of them anyway.

"By now," he said to the quiet audience, "you will have grasped from the newspaper that the Chauncey Line can no longer include Venus in its itinerary—but that is not such a cataclysmic disaster as you might suppose. The board and I have decided to include the other planets in our tours, which will about balance even with Manton. That is point one, and interesting though it is, it is not as interesting as an announcement in tonight's paper, which states that Manton is soon going to launch a machine which will definitely cure cancer. Such a machine, and others like it, will not be the property of hospitals, but of Manton himself—at his figure. That figure—need I say it—will be far beyond the reach of any average person. The benefit will only be felt by the wealthy sufferers, and the rank and file will be no better off."

"A typical Manton stunt in a Manton world," somebody commented drily.

"Yes—if Manton could get away with it," Nick responded. "It so happens that by a curious combination of circumstances I've got the whip-hand of him without ever intending to do so. The newspaper item states quite clearly that the basis of these cancer-destroying machines is a rare radioactive element. The exact name is not given, for obvious reasons, but I've checked on the fact that the element is entronium, obtainable only on Venus. How have I checked out that fact? That is what you're wondering?"

There was a nodding of heads but no remarks.

"My reason for saying that is that quite recently Manton stole every available speck of entronium from Venus—for which I took the blame. Hence, the boycotting of Venus to our space line—

though actually it was earlier thefts which started that. However, it is logical to assume that the theft of a huge quantity of entronium by Manton can only be for these machines. But I've got the entronium and I'm going to stick to it."

"And do what?" somebody asked. "Take a leaf out of Manton's book and sell the machines instead of him?"

"Not at all. Make the machines, stop him getting entronium so he can't do anything, and give the machines to the populace through the control of the hospitals."

"No money in that," somebody commented.

"No, but there's a vast amount of prestige for the Union of the Young, and a complete showing-up of Randle Manton and his money-grabbing ideas. We need a fillip after the beating we've taken on the space line, and this is our way of getting it."

"What about the machines themselves, Nick? Do you understand their construction?"

"Not in the least, but according to this report, they have been invented by a Dr. Welton, and Manton is financing them. The next thing I've got to do is get in touch with Welton and see what can be done. I have to have the authority of the Union to pay Welton an agreed sum for his basic idea. The building of the machines will be our own responsibility."

So began the arguments, back and forth, but after 30 minutes of hard talking Nick won his way—as usual. It was plain Manton was on the verge of launching a money-making racket out of people's suffering, and it was also plain that the Union of the Young needed something big to prove that they were in earnest.

The following day Nick went in search of Dr. Welton. It was no easy job to find him since he was not in the telephone or civic directory, but Nick finally managed through the Association of Scientists, of which body Welton proved to be a member. From there to the quaint old prewar house in Dorsay St. where Welton lived was only a short step.

The tired old scientist was courteous enough, and obviously interested as Nick vigorously outlined the reason for his visit.

"So that's the situation, doctor," he finished, spreading his hands. "What are you prepared to do about it?"

"Frankly, Mr. Chauncey, I don't see that there is much I can do. I've turned everything over to Randle Manton, for which I have received 1,000 credits as a kind of retainer. Later, when the machine is marketed, I shall receive a share of the profit. That is one of my conditions."

Nick smiled faintly. "Your machines will never be on the market, doctor, because I have the only supply of entronium. Without that, neither you nor Manton can move."

Welton was silent, running an indecisive finger down his cheek.

"Don't you think," Nick proceeded, "that you are entitled to a good deal more than a share of the profits? Don't you think you are entitled to recognition by the medical profession, together with whatever honors they are prepared to bestow on you, financial or otherwise?"

"Yes, but—" Welton smiled whimsically. "I'm afraid that beggars can't be choosers, Mr. Chauncey."

"You don't need to be a beggar if you listen to me instead of our go-getting friend Manton. You're a genius, in the same class as Lister, Pasteur and Roentgen. That genius needs acclaiming—and the Union of the Young wants acknowledging. And that is where we have got to get together... I'm suggesting that you give back Manton his 1,000 credits, reclaim your prints and designs, and turn everything over to me instead. As far as Manton is concerned, you have a good excuse. He isn't providing the entronium—and I know that he can't—and therefore you prefer to withdraw. If he demands a certain sum for the trouble he has been to in building machines, then turn the bill over to us and we'll deal with it."

Silence, as Welton struggled hard to make up his mind.

"You say he's paid you 1,000 credits, as a retainer. All right —we'll pay you 2,000 credits if you'll give back your 1,000 to Manton, and withdraw. You haven't signed any contract, have you?"

"Not yet—no."

"Very well, then; he has no hold over you. In the long run you'll be better off, as well as getting the acclaim of the masses."

"And would you allow me to take charge of the development of the machine? There are so many things it can do if I can only have unhampered movement to work out the details."

"Technically, the machine will be yours to do with as you will. You'll have 2,000 credits and all the awards that may be offered.

We, as the Union of the Young, are in effect your sponsors. That's the whole answer."

Welton pondered for a while, then he shrugged.

"Very well, Mr. Chauncey, I stand convinced. The thought that I can develop my system still further is what appeals to me."

Nick nodded and pulled out his cheque book. He wrote out a cheque for 2,000 credits and handed it across.

"There it is, doctor. All you have to do is sign this."

He added a foolscap sheet which he had withdrawn from his breast pocket. Welton looked through it and then nodded slowly.

"It's quite in order," Nick said. "It simply verifies that you are turning everything to us, and it gives you the necessary concessions for handling your own invention."

Welton did not delay any further. He appended his signature and then looked up.

"And Manton? Are you going to tell him or shall I?"

"In the first instance it had better come from you. If he raises any sort of trouble refer him to me and I'll take on the load."

So it was decided, and well satisfied with the arrangement Nick went on his way, prepared for the storm when it broke. But there was no storm. At first, when he heard from Welton, Manton was prepared to raise one, then he thought better of it. He had no legal hold over Welton, beyond the receipts for the diagrams and specifications he had lodged, and even this cancelled out when Welton sent back his 1,000 credits cheque. Welton did not say whom he was dealing with, but Manton knew perfectly well. He released Welton from his obligations with as good a grace as he could muster, while inwardly he smouldered at the defeat which had been inflicted on him. To inquire too closely into it, however, would have made entronium come into the limelight, and with things nicely balanced with Inva Krefel this would have been a fatal mistake.

"But if Chauncey thinks he's going to get away with this he's vastly mistaken," Manton muttered as he considered his position. "He's robbed me of a lucrative sideline, but two can play at that game. He'll get a beating in another direction, and before long, too!"

So while Manton plotted silently to avenge himself, Nick took on the handling of Welton's great idea. After the settlement of

Manton's bill for needless machines—paid by the Union of the Young through Welton—activity went ahead at full pressure. There was more than enough entronium to last for many years, all of which was transferred to a "radioactive bank" for safe keeping. By the time it ran out, Welton was convinced, another radioactive element in abundance would have been found.

This, however, was in the future. Immediate interest lay in the tests by the medical profession, and their delight in finding that the invention was all Dr. Welton claimed. It was put into immediate general service, and the credit was unhesitatingly given to Dr. Welton as the inventor, and the Union of the Young as his sponsor. As Nick had foreseen, the stock of the Union of the Young received a tremendous fillip, and the media—Manton's papers and t.v. stations excepted—was no longer so disparaging over the efforts of young people to try to pattern the post-war world.

"I confess," Welton said, as he discussed the matter in Nick's office some weeks later, "that I did a great deal of heart-searching when you came along with your offer, Mr. Chauncey. I need worry no more. The Welton machines are definitely established, and that is not all they are going to do, either."

Nick smiled. "Then you don't regard it as sufficient achievement that you have defeated the most malignant disease of mankind?"

"Not by any means. There are offshoots for the entronium treatment, as there are in every radioactive treatment. The atomic activity it possesses can he utilized in various ways. Especially in matters of the brain, for instance. I'm pretty sure that wavelength 70, as yet imperfectly examined, has the answer to congenital deafness, dumbness and blindness."

Nick started slightly. "Did you say blindness?"

"I did. Certain forms of it, that is. No machine on earth can possibly produce eyes where the eyes have been destroyed. That is a problem for the optical lens profession in conjunction with my machine...but in the case of brain defects I'm quite sure my machine can deal with them. Brain defects which have caused damage to the sight, I mean."

"Suppose," Nick said, "the case of a person with apparently perfect eyes—to look at, I mean—who has never seen because of radioactive radiation affecting the optic nerves and brain before birth. Could anything be done about that?"

Welton considered. "You mean a form of paralysis?"

"Yes. That's what it amounts to."

"I'll tell you that later. I've a lot of experimenting to do before I launch anything. Best thing I can do is advise you the moment I have anything worth while."

And with that Nick had to be content, but every time he thought of the possibility of giving Elise the one thing in life she wanted he glowed with pleasure, then succumbed to profound irritation at the time Welton seemed to take to make his experiments. Weeks passed, and nothing seemed to happen— though actually Welton was ceaselessly at work, aided, too, by all the best brains of the world of radioactivity and its application to the cure of humanity's ills.

It was also in these weeks that other matters demanded Nick's attention. His space line kept suffering reverses, a thing he could not afford with Manton's own line also in full action, subsidized by Inva Krefel. At root the reverses seemed normal enough, but when two machines crashed successively soon after take-off it did not seem that the business was purely accidental.

Nick investigated, and found nothing—or at least nothing tangible enough to provide him with legal proof. He discovered that the two machines which had crashed on the moon had been tampered with by the agents of Manton, but that was as far as he got. There was not enough evidence to publicly indict the big fellow.

"Something's got to be done." Nick muttered, as he surveyed the accounts. "This is Manton's genial way of hitting back because I beat him with that cancer machine racket, I suppose. Maybe I was a bit of a fool trying to benefit humanity without asking for any recompense. Every scrap of popularity which I built up for the Union of the Young has now about been wiped out and Manton is as strongly entrenched as he ever was...."

He ceased his muttering as the intercom buzzed. Impatiently he depressed the switch.

"Yes?"

"Dr. Welton is here, sir. Can he see you?"

"Definitely he can. Send him in."

Nick switched off and rose to greet the old scientist as he entered. He looked now as though life was treating him a good deal better than on the earlier occasions. He was smiling in quiet triumph, looked a good deal fatter, and was well dressed. In one hand he carried the inevitable briefcase.

"Glad to see you again, doctor," Nick said, pushing his personal worries on one side. "I was beginning to think you'd turned into a hermit."

"Anything but, Mr. Chauncey—anything but. You'll be glad to know that the cancer machines paid off handsomely. The medical profession made me a grant of some 5,000 credits a year in recognition of my services to the profession and humanity in general. I doubt if there is a cancer sufferer anywhere in the world now. If there is, rapid cure will come to them."

"Good," Nick said, reflecting that it was pleasant to hear of somebody making a success. "I'm glad the gamble paid off... But the blindness cure—you found that?"

"Of course I found it." Welton seemed surprised that the fact should even be doubted. "In any case, I knew it existed in the theoretical sense by very reason of entronium. It was simply a matter of pinning it down to practical use. That I have done, and made a machine. It works on blind and deaf animals, so there is no reason why it shouldn't work on a human being. That's why I'm here."

CHAPTER ELEVEN

And within half an hour Nick was on his way, with not one but two propositions in mind. Manton himself, all unaware of what was coming, was in the midst of conversation with Inva Krefel in the private office.

"I have to thank you, Excellency, for the way in which you have built up the space line," Manton was saying. "Thanks to inexplicable accidents to the Chauncey Line we now have everything in our favor. The machines are loaded to capacity."

The Venusian raised an eyebrow. "Did you say 'inexplicable', Mr. Manton?"

"So far as the public knows—and Chauncey, too—yes."

Manton grinned knowledgeably, and the Venusian shrugged his vast shoulders.

"You know your own business best, Mr. Manton. Naturally, the build-up of your space line has had a two-fold object. It helps me enormously with the commercial enterprises we have arranged between us, and it helps you in the same way... However the actual price of my aid to you—and I may say my continuing aid to you—has a higher price than any already paid."

"Oh?" Manton waited, the complacent grin vanishing from his face.

"I have decided that it would be beneficial to both of us if I married your daughter. If there should be any issue as a result of the union, the friendly relations between Venus and Earth would be all the more firmly cemented."

"Supposing—just supposing—she should refuse to marry you?"

"In that case I'm afraid we should have to terminate our very happy business relationship. Earth would not mean anything to me without an association with your daughter."

"Naturally, I do not expect any difficulty," Manton said. "I will have a talk with Elise tonight and let her see how much is at stake." Manton mused for a moment and then went on: "After all, she is as much a public servant as the one-time members of royalty were. If a marriage is to be of benefit all around—then she must make it—and I will not take no for an answer.... Rest assured, Excellency, everything will be in order."

The Venusian rose, bowed as he shook hands, and then departed. For a long time after he had gone, Manton stood at the window, scowling to himself .

"Don't like the situation a bit," he muttered. "That ugly brute as a son-in-law! And heaven knows how many tricks he'll pull once the marriage has taken place. Don't trust him. Wouldn't trust any Venusian any farther than I could kick him. It's a pity to have to subject Elise to this, but I don't see any other way..."

He paused, still pondering, then becoming vaguely aware that the morning light outside was dimmer than usual, he turned and switched on the office lights. A dim, distant rumble of thunder caught his ear. He reflected that he hadn't heard thunder since the war had ended. The weather had always been the same—dull gray, with no sun, and only very occasional rain.

The buzz of the intercom broke into his thoughts. Crossing to the instrument, he switched on.

"Yes? Manton speaking."

"Mr. Meredith of the weather bureau to see you, sir."

"Meredith? Oh, yes! Send him in."

In another moment the meteorologist had entered. Manton looked in surprise as he surveyed the tired face and the drawn lines about the eyes.

"Hello, Meredith. Been ages since I saw you. Have a seat."

"Thanks." Meredith sat down heavily. "I've come to warn you, Mr. Manton.... It's starting."

"Starting?" Manton's mind was on other things. "What's starting?"

"Have you looked at your barometer recently, or listened to the weather forecasts?"

"I'm too busy to listen to weather forecasts—and in any case we know what it's going to be—gray and rainy. As for the barometer—" Manton jerked himself to attention. "Why, yes! I remember you saying something about it. If it got very low or something."

Meredith nodded sombrely. "It's been landsliding for some days now—even weeks. Constantly dropping. At the moment it registers maximum zero."

"And what does that mean?"

"Trouble—and plenty of it. That trouble is starting now. You can hear it."

Manton listened for a moment to the distant rumbles of thunder and then, shading the glass from light reflection, he looked out of the windows. The sky was unpleasantly dark with a mass of clouds in the west rising like mountain ranges.

"The trouble is not local but world-wide," Meredith resumed. "The world charts show it, and presently the real waters will descend. I can only suggest one answer. Get away from the Earth as fast as possible."

Manton stared. "Get away from Earth? What the devil are you talking about?"

Meredith got to his feet and continued urgently: "It's the only way out, Mr. Manton. Before this business is ended this world of ours stands a 100-to-one chance of being transformed into a hydrosphere. Or in other words, a world composed of water. The people—as many as possible—must be flown to another planet. It's the only chance."

Manton shrugged. "Then it's impossible. My fleet is away in any case, on the trip to Venus. There isn't a machine on Earth at the moment."

"Then get Chauncey machines. The populace will demand it when they know what's coming."

"Who's to tell them? Only you. That would be idiotic. Might start a stampede."

"I shan't tell them anything: the government will do that. They know what's coming because the weather bureaus have told them."

Manton stood for a moment, trying to think. Lightning whiplashed the cavernous sky through the window as he pondered. The booming detonation of the thunder made him frown for a moment.

"Get out of here, Meredith," he said at last. "I've got to think this out. Pity you didn't tell me sooner."

"I've said it enough times on the radio and television—"

"Television! I've no time for that. You should have told me personally.... Go on—leave me alone."

Meredith shrugged and turned toward the door. When he got there he stopped and turned his haggard face.

"Good-bye sir," he said quietly. "I'm afraid I shan't be seeing you again."

Manton grunted something and then scowled. He sat at his desk and scowled some more. Finally he pulled out a cigar and snipped the end off.

"Depressing chap, Meredith," he muttered. "Shan't be seeing me again. Huh...."

The noise of the intercom as it burred seemed louder than usual, or else his nerves were on edge. Irritably he switched on.

"Yes? What is it?"

"Mr. Nicholas Chauncey to see you, sir. He says it's urgent."

Manton bit hard on his cigar. "Right. Send him in."

In a second or two Nick had entered the office. Manton did not get up. He sat gazing uncompromisingly.

"Well, Chauncey, what do you want? Or don't you know you're not welcome in my office?"

"I hardly expected the red carpet to be out," Nick replied. "I want to discuss a business deal with you."

"Business deal with me? Evidently this is my morning tor surprises. Take a seat."

Nick did so, waited until a crack of thunder had subsided, and then came to the point.

"I know perfectly well that your agents have caused two of my machines to smash on the moon, and that you have had rumors circulated as to the insecurity of my line—but I can't do anything because I've no real proof," Nick said. "So, there it is. You can add my fleet to your own and become sole owner of the only space line in existence."

"How many machines have you got?" Manton asked.

"About 80, and since you know what they're like I don't need to describe them."

"And what's your price?"

"One million credits, which includes the few tourists already booked."

Manton smiled grimly. "I'll give you 500,000 credits for the lot, incuding your executive headquarters. That's all junk is worth to me."

"I suppose you're offering that disgusting figure because there is nobody else who will be interested in my offer?"

"I'm offering all I intend to, Chauncey. Take it or leave it."

"I'll leave it," Nick said, surprisingly. "I don't want a liability on my hands, but at the same time I don't intend to sell at such a crippling loss." He got to his feet. "Sorry we couldn't do business—"

"Not so hasty," Manton placated gently, remembering still the words of Meredith. "Let's say 750,000."

Nick strode actively toward the door, and before Manton could think of anything more to say the door had closed. He sat down slowly compressing his lips. Those extra machines would have been enormously useful if things came to a crisis. A pity Nick Chauncey was so tough to get along with.

CHAPTER TWELVE

In a matter of minutes Nick Chauncey's fast convertible covered the distance through the city to the Manton residence. It was like driving at night, except for the constant glaring of lightning. Nick's headlamps were in full blaze as he swept up the drive of the residence and then jammed on the brakes.

The manservant, unmoved as ever, opened the door. The light of the hall lamp shone out from behind him.

"Nicholas Chauncey's the name," Nick said. "I wish to see Miss Manton right away. Urgent business."

"If you will step inside, sir?"

Nick did so and waited impatiently as the manservant moved calmly to one of the many rooms leading off the hall. Then at length he returned with the same grave composure.

"If you will come this way, sir?"

Nick obeyed promptly, to presently find himself ushered into an enormous library. It was almost in darkness except for lightning, and at the desk Elise sat, busy with some kind of card index. Nick wondered why he had not realized she did not need the light to do her work. Then the door closed behind him.

"Yes, Nick, what is it?" Elise raised her head and sat waiting for his answer.

He went closer, blinking for a moment as a savage flash dazzled him. When the concussions had subsided he spoke quietly.

"I want you to come up town with me, Elise, to hear about something that will do you a great deal of good. A cure for your blindness—"

"I'm not interested. There is no cure. You should know that."

Nick watched her for a moment, then gazed through the window. In the gloom he saw part of the grounds and beyond them the drive and his car. Quietly he made up his mind.

"Sorry, Elise, for what's going to happen," he said. "It's for your own good."

She rose from her chair in surprise and at that moment Nick's fist struck her violently under the jaw. Without a word her limp body pitched forward into his waiting arms.

Nick wasted no time after that. Sweeping the unconscious girl into a firmer grip, he unlatched and opened the french window and then sped swiftly through the gloom toward the drive. Twice lightning forked the sky as he went, but he felt reasonably sure that he had not been seen.

Finally Nick gained the Welton Clinical Laboratory on Third Ave., a biggish place and alive with lights. Scooping Elise up into his arms, he entered the hallway and went over to the reception desk.

"I'm Nick Chauncey," he announced to the surprised sister in charge. "Dr. Welton's expecting me. Hurry—if you please."

Convinced of the urgency by the limp girl lying in Chauncey's arms the sister wasted no time, and in a few moments Nick found himself walking into Welton's private laboratory. He put Elise down carefully on one of the long stretcher-tables and then relaxed a trifle.

"I've brought your subject, doc," he said, shaking hands. "She didn't seem inclined of her own free will, so I had to use a little persuasion."

Elise began to show signs of returning consciousness. Nick moved slowly toward her, and Welton stood watching intently.

"Okay, take it easy," Nick said quietly, as the girl's eyelids opened. "I knocked you out, and I'm darned sorry I had to do it. It was essential, though."

Elise slowly sat up, with Nick's arm behind her shoulders. She listened for a moment to the booming thunder and then frowned a little and felt her throbbing jaw.

"What's it all about, Nick?" she demanded, gripping his hand. "I know I'm safe with you, but I've never known you to behave like this before. What's it for?"

"At the moment, dearest, you're in Dr. Welton's clinic. That perhaps doesn't mean anything to you, but he's—"

"But it does! Isn't he the scientist who discovered the cure for cancer? The one who let dad down?"

"He discovered the cancer cure, yes—and he didn't let anybody down. Anyway, that doesn't signify at the moment. Dr. Welton has other strings to his bow besides the cure of cancer, and the cure of certain forms of blindness is one of them."

Elise was silent, debating what Nick had told her.

"Perfectly true, Miss Manton," Welton said. "When I mentioned the fact to Mr. Chauncey he immediately described your case—and the problem of partial brain paralysis is a problem no longer. My instruments can instantly dispose of it."

Welton moved quietly and methodically, pushing a wheeled machine from a corner of the laboratory. It looked rather like a very elaborate cine-camera and had a multitude of varicolored wires attached to insulators and leading back to a stout cable connected to a small generator. Finally Welton had it in position and snapped a switch. The generator hummed softly.

"Now," Welton murmured. "Raise your face a little, Miss Manton. There—that's it." He tipped her chin gently. "Don't move from that position. Ready?"

"Yes, ready," Elise assented huskily.

Welton fingered a variety of plugs and buttons on the apparatus. Once or twice he winced as brilliant flashes of lightning seemed to come right into the laboratory, followed by a stunning concussion of sound. Elise, too, must have heard the appalling noise of the storm but she did not shift position... Then presently she sensed a gentle warmth lying across her face from ear to ear.

For the rest, it was simply a confirmation of the miracle she was expecting. By gradual degrees the darkness to which she was accustomed became shot through with bars and running dots of light. And to the dots color became added, those colors which nobody had been able to describe to her.... Dots and bars, shafts of color, then a twisting and turning of the remaining lines of shadow. Everything looked as though she were gazing through a sheet of glass down which colored liquids were streaming. But only for a moment. The streaming ceased in a whirl of dazzling lights and the picture became steady.

Everything was forgotten for the moment. Even the booming of the storm. Elise turned her head slowly, drinking in the wonder of her new faculty—and at last she looked at Nick. He did not need to ask her if the experiment had succeeded. Her eyes were looking right at him and not through him, and they were brimming with tears.

"Nick..." she whispered, surrendering herself to his arms. "Oh, Nick...."

*   *   *

The storm centre which had struck London was only, in actual fact, the fringe of vastly greater storms which were developing in intensity with every hour over the European continent. First, as in London, had come the initial air disturbances in the outbursts of thunder and lightning, then these had given way to rain and wind, mounting through the hours, and sweeping in a gigantic storm area in the general direction of London.

Thus it was that by mid-morning Randle Manton found himself on the line with the prime minister. His strained, urgent voice came over the wire like somebody speaking from another world.

"Mr. Manton, how many spaceships have you available at the moment?"

"None," Manton answered cryptically. "Nor can I get at them. Storm interference has cut off radio contact. Why do you ask?"

"I have been warned by the weather bureau that there is serious trouble developing climatically, which in the end may kill many thousands of people. There is no safe spot on Earth—or at least there won't be before long. The only solution is evacuation to another world—Venus, if it can be arranged—until the disturbances are over."

Manton laughed shortly. "I'm afraid that you are allowing yourself to be stampeded, Mr. Prime Minister. It's a long way from a violent storm to the end of the world. I know how persistent these weathermen are. I've had one here full of dark forebodings. I should forget all about the business."

"If I could do that, Mr. Manton, I'd be only too glad—but I have a responsibility to the country, along with the government. If there should be disaster, the government will be the first to get the blame for not being prepared.... And you have no vessels at all?"

"None. Every one is in service."

"Have you any idea how the Chauncey Line is fixed?"

Manton bristled. "I don't know, sir—and I might add that I don't care. Sorry I can't help you. Good-bye."

Disgruntled, and vaguely unnerved, he returned to his work—or tried to. Hardly had he got started than the office door opened and Elise and Nick came in, both of them carrying a glitter of raindrops on their clothes. In amazement Manton sat staring at them.

"Why the devil don't you announce yourself, Chauncey?" he demanded. "You come bursting into my office like—"

"Never mind that, dad," Elise interrupted, hurrying forward. "It was me who was responsible for bursting in. Can't you tell there is something different about me? Look at me!"

Manton looked puzzled. "Well, what's different?" he demanded, and Elise laughed.

"Suppose I told you that your tie isn't straight? Suppose I said that your face is just what I'd imagined it would be like. Suppose I told you—"

"Wait! Wait a minute, girl!" Manton surged out of his chair and gripped her shoulders tightly. "Let me look at you, Elise!"

She remained passive in his grip. For a long moment he looked into her face.

"You—you can see!" he whispered, and she nodded emphatically.

"For the first time in my life, and I owe it all to Nick, and to Dr. Welton."

"Thank God," Manton muttered, drawing the girl tightly to him and kissing her gently. "Whatever the explanation, or the machinations behind it, thank God that you are cured. The one thing I had always wanted to give you, my dear, and always it seemed to elude me." ·

The intercom interrupted Manton. He pressed down the switch. "Yes, what is it?"

"His Excellency Inva Krefel to see you urgently, Mr. Manton."

Elise started, and Nick gave a grim smile. For a moment Manton was at a loss—but only for a moment.

"I'll see him," he said quietly, and as he switched off his mind reverted to the task he had promised to undertake. To ask Elise if she would consent to marrying the giant Venusian. But now things were immeasurably altered.... His eyes strayed across to her. She was fixedly watching the office door.

Then the door opened and the Venusian came slowly in, shedding a shower of raindrops in his passage. He glanced about him, inclined his head to Nick, gave Elise the briefest glance, then went right over to Manton.

"An early return, Excellency," Manton commented.

"Forced upon me by necessity, Mr. Manton, I assure you...." The Venusian turned, "Good morning, Elise—my felicitations to you."

Elise did not answer. She stared fixedly, so fixedly indeed that Krefel evidently assumed her blindness was the cause. He turned back to Manton.

"I have been listening in my hotel to the emergency broadcasts, Mr. Manton, and it appears that there is very real danger in this world of yours. Though I do not scientifically understand it, I gather that a Girdle of Waters is descending from the upper heights to the lower levels, and may well produce a flood. It may happen at any moment. That being so, I don't intend to delay my stay on Earth here. I have decided to return to Venus with my entourage, and I wish to take your daughter with me... Or perhaps you have not had the time yet to discuss matters with her?"

Elise interrupted with a queer, half-strangled sound. It was partly an exclamation, and partly an expression of utter disgust. She turned abruptly, dashed for the anteroom door, and snatched it open. The door slammed behind her.

"Am I to understand from that reaction, Mr. Manton, that your daughter no longer wishes to associate with me?"

"I can't imagine anything plainer," Manton replied.

"You realize what this means, of course? Complete severance of all interests between us, withdrawal of all subsidies in regard to money, and a complete boycott of Venus to Earthlings for as long as I am in control of the planet?"

"Yes, I realize it," Manton sighed. "Even so, tough though it is for me, it's better than selling my daughter in order to get extra power. I was trying to find the answer after you came this morning. I've found it—unexpectedly."

The Venusian tossed his head angrily. "That being the case, I will depart, Mr. Manton. The tourists you have sent to Venus you will have back quickly—and they will never come again. All I need is a space ship to return home."

"I have none. I'm afraid you must wait until the fleet returns."

The Venusian smouldered in silence for a moment or two; then he turned sharply on Nick.

"You have machines, Mr. Chauncey?"

"A small fleet," Nick agreed drily.

"Then I will use one of yours, and I want it within an hour."

Nick shrugged. "Sorry I can't oblige you, Excellency. As the controller of the Chauncey Line I still have the last word as to whom I shall take as passengers. I have a variety of reasons for refusing you permission. One reason is that you backed the Manton Line against mine; and the other reason is that you accused me of a theft in which I had no part."

"If the situation calls for action, Mr. Chauncey, you'll most certainly get it!" Krefel said flatly—and with that he left the office. The slam he gave to the door was the sole indication of his towering rage.

Slowly Manton and Nick turned to look at one another. Down the windows, against the night-black sky, rain was pouring with relentless fury.

"Mind if I use your phone?" Nick asked after a moment, and Manton briefly indicated it as he crossed to the window and stared outside.

"That you, Harry?" Nick's voice asked presently. "Listen, this is important. Double the guard round the spaceport watch-tower points, and tell them not to pull their punches if there's any trouble. I expect some, mainly from Venusian Inva Krefel. Got that clear?"

Nick hung on to the phone for a moment or two, then with a brief "Okay! Good-bye," he put the instrument down.

"So Krefel doesn't get any of your machines at any price?" Manton asked, turning.

He seemed about to say something further when the door of the anteroom clicked and Elise came into view. She looked briefly about her.

"Has he gone?' she inquired, coming forward.

"For good," Manton said, his arm going about her shoulders as she reached his side. "And with him he's taken the bulk of my business and cut off all chances of a fortune in trade. I'm inclined to think that Manton's world is a little cock-eyed at the moment. If anybody's got anything out of this post-war chaos it would appear to be Nick Chauncey here. At least he's got a space line he can build up again. I shan't be able to with so many other financial entanglements to see to."

"How much did you lose, dad, through not doing things as Krefel expected?"

"Materially I lost a good deal, but in return I have you—and the young man who has been instrumental in restoring you to normal."

Nick looked up in surprise. "That sounds quite strange, coming from you, Mr. Manton."

"I don't know why it should. In case you don't know it, I have feelings the same as anybody else. I'll always be grateful for what you've done for Elise, but that doesn't say I agree with your ideas in general. Now look, regarding this space line of yours, I think—"

"That can wait," Elise interrupted. "I've got something to say about things. We're going right home, the three of us, and tell mother the good news. Forget all about your business competition and do something natural for a change. Right?"

Nick smiled rather sheepishly and Manton hesitated. Then he grinned.

"Home it is," he assented. "Let's go."

Manton stepped out into gloom and the waters came up over his knees. He held up his powerful arms.

"Okay, Elise—piggy-back," he said, and the girl did not ask any questions but submitted herself to his strong grip. Through the flooded streets he went and then commenced the difficult, slippery journey toward the darkened house, rain pelting in sheets around him, and Nick sloshing through the water a few feet in the rear.

Jackson, the manservent, was not quite in such control of himself as he opened the hall doorway. Behind him an emergency battery light glowed like a yellow eye as he peered into the rain-washed dark.

"Great heavens, sir—it's you!" he ejaculated.

"Glad you recognize me," Manton growled, setting Elise on her feet. "Where's my wife? How's things here?"

"The mistress is in the lounge, sir. Things here are a bit out of order. Lighting and power have failed, so I switched in the emergency circuit. All the staff has deserted, sir. They seemed afraid of the storm and wanted to get away."

Manton sniffed and tossed back his rain-dripping hair. "Herd instinct, I suppose. Thanks for staying behind, Jackson. I shall not forget that."

"Thank you, sir." Jackson looked rather wonderingly as Elise, her clothes plastered to her like a swimsuit, hurried over toward the lounge and vanished inside it.

They hurried into the lounge, to find Ann Manton in the midst of embracing her daughter. Manton stood aside for a moment from the emotional scene, then at length Ann looked up at him with tears in her eyes.

"Randle," she whispered, "Elise has been telling me all about it. This is the most wonderful thing that ever happened."

"Definitely so, my dear." Manton moved forward and took her outstretched hand in his. For a moment all three of them were quiet, but the mental bond that existed between them was profound. Nick, apart from the three, surveyed them in the dull light of the emergency lamps. Manton, soaked and tousled, his craggy face half smiling and Elise looking very much like a younger edition of her mother with tears glinting in her eyes.

Then abruptly Manton was in command again. He had little time for prolonged sentimentality.

"As you'll have observed," he said, "there is something wrong with the weather, and if I am to believe an expert in these matters, there's a lot of trouble coming. How we get out of it I don't know. Apparently the safest thing to do would be to leave the earth altogether until things settled down—"

"Might we try the radio and see if there's any guide as to what's happening?" Elise remarked, and as her father nodded she headed over to it and switched on.

They listened as the voice of the announcer came through.

"...of evacuation from the central areas. The government is taking immediate steps to commandeer all space machines so that people important to the community can be safe during the approaching upheaval. News from other countries is very sparse owing to the climatic conditions, but it seems—"

Manton strode across and switched the radio off. He gave Nick a grim look.

"You heard what he said, Nick? The government is going to take all space machines for the evacuation of the high and mighty! That means your machines. I haven't got any; not here anyhow."

"Then you're proposing co-operation between us?" Nick asked.

"I am. Reason it out for yourself. The world I built up is collapsing. The ideals of your Union of the Young have collapsed too, for the same reason. If you and I ever get out of this alive, we'll need both maturity and youth to build something new—an alliance of my generation and yours, in what's left of your Union. Even then we'll have to fight like the devil to get a foothold—but at least we'll fight together because Elise will see that we do. She's like the cement to hold things in place. What do you say?"

"I'm with you," Nick agreed.

CHAPTER THIRTEEN

In a very short space of time Ann, Elise and Jackson were all ready, each one carrying a small valise. Manton looked them over and nodded.

"Good enough—"

"I've packed some stuff for you as well, Randle," Ann said. "You didn't mention it, but I did it just the same."

He grinned faintly. "Good. I forgot about that. What about you, Nick? Want to call in home?"

"No, thanks. Nobody there anyhow, and there's a change of clothes in all the space machines. I'll get by. Come on! I'll feel safer once we get going."

They delayed only long enough for Manton to cut off the electric supply at the mains, then they hurried out under the black sky to his helicopter. Wind snatched at them as they went, sending them staggering with each buffeting gust, but finally they gained the helicopter's cabin and sealed themselves in. As the owner, Manton took the controls and whisked them into the agitated air.

Swaying slightly in the gusts, Manton brought the helicopter down on the space ground itself and then opened the cabin door. He clambered out and assisted Ann and Elise down after him. Then came Jackson and Nick.

Nick moved immediately to the office marked "Embarkation Control" and passed inside. Manton followed him a second or two later.

"Any inquiries for Mr. Manton?" he questioned.

"Yes, sir. There are two gentlemen waiting in Anteroom four—names of Welton and Sedberg."

"Right. Have them told we're here," Nick ordered; then when the official had finished with the intercom he went on, "How have things been here? Were my instructions carried out to defend this airport against possible attack?"

"Yes, Mr. Chauncey. I'm afraid there has been a bit of trouble, but I didn't know where to get in touch with you for orders."

Nick's face hardened. "What kind of trouble?"

"From Krefel, the Venusian—even as you intimated. He and his men arrived and demanded a spaceship. When it was refused they used armed force, and devilishly queer weapons they had, too! Two of our boys were killed and Krefel and his entourage got to one of the machines and took off."

"Then?" Nick snapped.

"It happened. Either they didn't know how to control the thing, or else it was atmospheric disturbance—I don't know. Anyhow, they crashed from about 30,000 feet. We only finished a little while ago removing the bodies. They're in the hospital ward at the moment."

"Dead?" Nick asked. "Or just injured!"

"Dead—the lot of them."

"Right. Now listen, Harry—" he turned to the official. "Send out a general warning of what's coming, then figure out for yourself how best to use what spaceships we have here. If you can't do that, use whatever cover you can. I've got one ship I'm using, for Manton, his wife and daughter, and these other two men who are important to the community. Okay?"

"Okay, sir."

Nick shook hands briefly, then hurried across to where Manton was greeting the aged Dr. Welton and the somewhat bewildered Sedberg as they emerged from an adjoining anteroom.

"Got the plans of your health machines, Welton?" Manton asked quickly, and the scientist shook his head.

"No. Mr. Manton. I didn't know they were wanted. Anyway, my dealings are with Mr. Chauncey—"

"We're in partnership. How long will it take to get them?"

"I don't need to. I can do everything from memory."

"Better still.... What about you, Sedberg? Any special plans you want to collect for future use? You're going to be important if there's any world left in the future."

"My memory's good enough," the rocket engineer replied.

"Then we're ready," Manton said. "Right, Nick?"

Nick did not need to answer. He opened the main door and then went reeling at the blast of screaming air which struck him. Somehow he saved himself by clinging on to a door pillar; then he fought his way back to Ann and Elise as they stood waiting on the threshold.

"All of us make a chain!" he yelled. "The only way!"

Promptly, the seven of them linked arms and then plunged into the blinding fury of the storm. Rain had started again, and this added to the tearing, wrenching wind which made it nearly impossible to see as they blundered and swayed across the tarmac. Even as they went, several of the tall floodlight pillars splintered and crashed, the lamps splintering into darkness after a flaring of short-circuited wires.

Individually, they could never have covered the distance, but collectively their weight kept them on the ground and so they gained the nearest of the grounded space machines. One by one they crawled inside, then Nick crossed to the switch which closed the airlock. Immediately all external sound ceased, but the machine was rocking precariously under the ever growing fury of the hurricane.

"Get going—quick!" Manton panted, staring through the observation window. "Take a look out here..."

Seven anxious faces peered into the wild darkness of rain outside. Then momentarily, lighted by a brilliant flash of forked lighting, they saw something. It looked like a level mountain range racing out of the night. Level, and yet with its top curiously sawlike. Possibly it was some seven or eight miles away.

"Tidal wave!" Nick gulped, activating switches. "And what a wave! It must be nearly 1,000 feet high..."

His eyes jumped to the switch panel. The moment the gauges showed a full power reading he closed the circuit levers and gave the space machine almost half power. It lurched violently and then lifted, hurtling through the maddened air with terrific velocity.

Half paralyzed with the gravitational drag and fear of destruction the seven lay supine on their bunks, everything outside blotted out by swirling mists and yellow vapors. Time and again the appalling wind swung the machine out of its course, but so tremendous was its upward escape velocity that it kept on going... and going.

Until suddenly there was no more vapor. Only the dazzling light of the unmasked sun and the infinite blackness of space with the baleful glitter of the stars.

"We did it," Manton muttered. "Just in time."

For nearly a week the space machine cruised close to the Earth, the travellers watching anxiously in between their sleeping periods for some sign of a break in Earth's cloud canopy. It came at last, to give a view of ocean through the clouds. Only then did Nick think it safe to descend for a closer look.

So the space machine returned, landing finally on what appeared to be a small rocky plateau, lashed by the waves of a mountainous sea. Clouds were thick and heavy, but only of the type one might expect on a rainy, blustering day.

In silence the seven gazed out on the dreary scene.

"Where are we?" Manton asked at last.

"Should be England," Nick said. "Some part of it."

"This," said Elise, staring intently out of the window, "is the world of water which I saw in my vision. I recognize it."

"All that remains of the world you built up, Randle," Ann murmured, laying a hand on his arm. "Now you have the proof, I ask you: was it worth it?"

"On the face of it, no," he replied. "But out of it I have found Dr. Welton, one of the greatest benefactors ever known as far as human suffering is concerned. Again, I found Nick Chauncey, about the most suitable husband Elise could have, and a future power-in-the-land.... There'll be another world in time, once the waters abate, maybe jointly controlled by men and women just in case the male sex gets out of hand."

The men grinned as Nick reached to the airlock switch. Then he paused as Elise caught his arm and pointed excitedly.

"Look! All of you! On that cloud! I've often wondered what it looked like, and at last I know."

They were all silent for a moment, looking intently as a shaft of sunlight came streaming down and patterned itself on the opposite storm cloud.

There, in all its radiant glory, arched a rainbow.

CHAPTER I

THE CELESTIAL SHOW

THAT extraordinarily rare event, the impending collision of two stars, was quite sufficient to stir the scientifically minded of the world's peoples to considerable interest in the late September of that fateful year when the possibility was announced by the leading astronomers.

Unfortunately, the occurrence would be so distant as to be hardly visible to the unaided eye—a momentary flash of light, perhaps, if one knew exactly where to look for it. In actual fact, paradoxically enough, the event had already happened, but so vast was the distance, the light waves from the occurrence were only just appearing—past images of an event long gone.

The main thing was that here was a chance, by the purchase of a small telescope or good field glasses—manufactured by the millions by enterprising firms—to see Nature in a mood never before known. Or at least never seen since the Earth itself had been created, and even at Earth's creation there had not been an actual collision, only a passing of two stars—the sun and a runaway.

Obviously, the only accurate recording of such an event would have to be made in space itself, where, unhindered by atmosphere and equipped with the finest telephoto plates, a full recording of the event could be made, together with a complete motion film.

Automatically the assignment fell to Space Enterprises, Incorporated, the only space-travelling company in the world, in which were merged countless other businesses and a multitude of famous names. The Company's ships plied regularly from Earth to all the worlds of the system in search of valuable minerals, ores, materials that would give one man power over another. Every planet was devoid of life, that fact was proven. Therefore, the

Company's sole work was commercial...

Blake Venner, ace pilot of the void, was more than satisfied with the assignment. In fact, he spent the whole evening before his departure raving about it to Sheila Berick, daughter of the Company's President. Because she loved Blake well enough to be engaged to him, she listened dutifully, calmed him down gently whenever his excitable nature got the better of him.

Even so, he paced the warm luxury of the girl's fashionable New York apartment and persistently refused her offers to sit down beside her on the divan.

"Think of it!" he cried, his bright blue eyes gleaming and his wiry fair hair standing up in an obstinate tuft. "A terrific contribution to science! A movie film of something that's never happened in history before—to our knowledge, that is. What a gift to hand to posterity! Celestial collision! Say, did you ever read up on Jeans?" he asked quickly, turning.

Sheila nodded her dark head slowly. "Of course..." Her brown eyes were faintly amused. "Why?"

"Remember *The Mysterious Universe*?" Blake finally accepted the offer to sit beside her. "If I remember rightly, Jeans said it is an 'unimaginable rarity' for one star to come anywhere near another star. Then he gives that excellent analogy of his. He pictures a scale model in which the stars are ships, and by this means each ship is found to be at least a million miles from its nearest neighbour; showing thereby the rarity of even close approach, let alone a collision. Yet, two thousand million years ago this occurrence took place, and the solar system was born. From then until now, there have been no such coincidences... But now, judging purely, of course, from the light waves hurtling across space, a runaway star out beyond Alpha Centauri will collide with Egusus 612, a small dwarf type star not unlike our own sun."

"You're making me envious," the girl smiled. "It should be a sight for the gods right out in space."

"Your father won't let you come then?" Blake asked.

"No—against regulations; and you know what Dad is for upholding regulations. I tried all my wiles on him, but it just wouldn't work... so you see, even the President's daughter gets no favours. Maybe I'll think of something else," she finished, smiling again.

Blake shrugged. "It's tough, but I suppose it's only right. Space is no picnic, even for a trained man..." He relapsed into thought for a moment, then his face brightened again. "Well anyway, once this assignment's over; I'm due for two month's vacation. Are you still enough in love with a lunatic to marry me?"

"Nothing can change that!" There was no hesitation in the girl's answer. For all his impulsiveness, she knew Blake's sterling qualities, his reckless courage. For a moment her dark eyes studied his somewhat pugnacious features, then she said quietly, "I'll be waiting here for you when you get back, and I'll bet there'll be plenty of lionising and feting for you and Nick. It isn't every day that two pilots secure such a scoop as has fallen to you two. In the interval, I'll record everything in my diary; it will help me to keep in touch with you even though you're millions of miles away in space."

Blake shook his head in mystification. "That diary of yours should make good reading one day—or rather diaries. You've been at it for years now, haven't you...?"

He broke off as his gaze caught the clock. Vigorously, he got to his feet, buttoned up his uniform collar.

"I guess time always goes by too fast when I'm with you. Got to turn in early tonight. We leave at eight in the morning and will be away about two weeks or so. The collision takes place a week from today at 8.13 in the evening. You'll be watching it?"

Sheila rose to her feet, her satin gown clinging to her slender form. She did not answer the question.

"I suppose," she said slowly, "that I'll have to buy a telescope and watch, if all else fails. I did so want to see the collision from space."

"Forget it," Blake smiled. "Your dad's right. You'd feel cockeyed for weeks after the journey." He stooped, kissed her gently. "Take care of yourself," he murmured, then suddenly releasing her, he strode lithely to the door...

BY 8.15 the following morning, the Space Enterprises' finest equipped and fastest machine was clear of the stratosphere, plunging at ever increasing speed through the clear reaches of infinity, driven onwards against Earth's gravitational field by the powerful Bennett-Jones *dilinite* rocket fuel. Ahead loomed the always incomprehensibly vastness of space, studded with the nearer view of the inner planets and moon, the distant dimensionless glittering of the stars.

Blake sat squarely in his padded chair, hands on the controls, eyes on his instruments. Behind him, checking over the apparatus, was Nick Vane, by far the smartest scientist the Company possessed.

Tall, sallow skinned and dark, he took life with a certain immovable gravity; he was the kind of man who would remain undisturbed through an earthquake and would record the effects in copper plate handwriting. He and Blake made an excellent team; they were the firmest of friends, the one courageous and impulsive and the other calculating and impassive. Their joint efforts had never yet failed to produce perfect results.

"I wonder," Nick said presently, "if we're heading right into a death trap..."

"Huh?" Blake looked up, startled. "You're a nice cheerful sort of guy to go around with. What do you mean, anyhow?"

"I'm considering the possibilities, and the more I consider, the more I wonder. Maybe there are things we didn't have the time to check up on. For instance, the collision of two stars will produce intense bursts of radiation of various sorts, and plenty of them may never have happened before. Because they travel at the speed of light, they'll reach us identically at the same moment we see the collision... I wonder what will happen then?"

"What the hell *can* happen?" Blake snorted. "Throwing a scare into me like that! You know as well as I do that this ship's proofed against all radiation in three separate sections. Even cosmic rays can't get through, and they're about the most powerful thing of all we're likely to contend with."

Nick shrugged. "Well, it was only a consideration, anyway. I like to weigh the possibilities of everything from the very start. If I'm going to die, I prefer to know in what fashion—"

"Yeah, including the colour of your coffin and the date of burial?" Blake finished drily. "If you'd forget your passion for organization for a moment, the trip would be a lot, happier for me! You're putting me right off my stroke."

"Sorry!" Nick grinned a little. "Maybe I am wrong at that."

Whether he considered the matter further or not, he did not

mention it again. For a week of earth-time, the vessel flew onwards under Blake's skilful guidance, travelled well out beyond Pluto into the real abysmal depths of space by the time the pre-calculated moment for the collision arrived.

With the automatic pilot in operation, both men gave their full attention to the void and the drama being enacted there. It was quite enough to make Nick gaze in admiring wonder. To the split second, Egusus 612 and the runaway unknown, both of them stars of the sun's diameter, united in a common blast of unbearable brilliance.

The movie telephoto cameras ground out steadily, recording every detail. Nick busied himself with the still-plate apparatus. Blake glanced at the self-registering instruments recording all that was necessary in the scientific line—brilliance of light emitted, displacement of mean position, and so forth.

At last the two stars had coalesced into a common oneness. The brilliance of the impact was dying. The two would probably condense into one white dwarf of incredible heaviness. The show was over.

"Hmm..." Nick commented. "Seems an awful distance to come for such a short display, especially when everybody else will see it in comfort at the television theatres. Ah well, I suppose that's what mugs like us are for! Turn her round, Blake, and let's get home!"

He unfastened the film cans with a practised hand, moved into the adjoining dark room, and closed the door.

CHAPTER II

DESERTED WORLD

EIGHT days later the return journey was almost complete. Earth loomed green and resplendent from the depths of the void— first a cloud-wreathed globe, then becoming flat as the space ship dropped through the clouds with fast-diminishing speed.

As usual, Blake watched his instruments carefully, studied the ground-reflecting screens.

Presently the faintest hint of a frown crossed his face.

"Say!" he exclaimed, looking up, "I'd rather expected some sort of demonstration on our return, hadn't you? Not that I want it, of course, only it seemed inevitable. Queer, don't you think, that there's nobody around?"

"I agree."

Nick's brows came down. The ship was well below the clouds now, dropping directly over New York, heading west of the city for the open landing grounds encompassed in the horseshoe-shaped Enterprise Building.

But certainly there was nobody in sight in all that great expanse —no waiting crowds—not even the usual army of mechanics waiting to receive the flyer.

Blake's frown deepened. He snapped on the radio sharply.

"Blake Venner calling Enterprise!" he intoned. "Prepare to receive ship. All O.K. down there?"

There was no response—in fact no sound whatever save the throb of the powerful underjets braking the ship's fall.

Nick stared at the radio fixedly, disbelief on his features.

"Hello there!" Blake barked. "What's wrong down there? Answer my signal, can't you?"

The radio remained mute. Blake glanced up in genuine concern.

"Something decidedly wrong here, Nick," he breathed. "I don't like it! Where the devil *is* everybody?"

Nick remained silent, frowning in slow bewilderment. By slow degrees, the ship settled gently. Blake switched off the engines and regarded Nick for a moment in the heavy silence that ensued.

"Well, might as well see what it's all about," Nick remarked at length, and going over to the airlock, he unfastened the clamps.

Thoughtfully, he stepped out onto the tarmac and stood gazing around. The cool autumnal wind blew around him, gloriously fresh after the stifling artificiality of the space ship.

His dark, perplexed eyes gradually moved the length of the semicircular Enterprise Building, along its myriad windows and doorways. Suddenly he came to a decision, began to walk across the space towards the massive main entrance. Blake caught him up in a moment.

"I don't like this silence," he muttered, and he found himself involuntarily walking on tiptoe. "You've noticed it? No birds singing, no rumble of traffic—no anything, in fact. It's just like a cemetery!"

"Uh-huh," Nick acknowledged, pondering—and they went up the broad granite steps together.

Their footsteps echoed oddly in the immense space with its lofty domed roof of glass. Normally this entrance hall should have been seething with activity—officials, booking clerks, scientists and technicians.

But now—nobody!

Everything was still, in a state of curious disorder as though everybody had left in a hurry. The clerks' desks were in their places as usual, ledgers still open upon them. The main staff elevator was level with the floor, with its gates flung wide open.

"Look!" Blake whispered, and pointed behind him. His and Nick's feet had left distinct marks in a gathered film of dust.

For many days not a soul had passed in or out of this normal hive of industry.

Nick pursed his lips, traced his finger across the nearest desk. Behind his finger streaked a long bright line of polished mahogany. He looked at Blake in bafflement, then with one accord they moved to the elevator and pressed the button. Nothing happened; the power was off. Still in silence, they mounted the stairs, walked along the endless corridors and stared into the rooms wherein lay the space pilots' quarters. Nobody was in sight. In the pilots' mess, a gigantic room for general assemblage, there was the usual appearance of disorder and not a soul around.

And the silence! It began to get on Blake's nerves when they had finished the touring and came back again to the front steps. They gazed over the deserted tarmac towards their spaceship, across at the locked hangars where the rest of the space machines were housed.

Nick moved away suddenly, went across to the hangar doors and slid aside the watchman's inspection plate. After a moment or two, he rejoined Blake.

"Hangars are full," he commented briefly. "Thought perhaps a sudden space-expedition might account for this."

Again they went quiet—gazing at the empty sky, oppressed by the pall of silence.

"Queer!" Nick commented at last.

Blake swung to him. "Queer!" he echoed. "Good God, man, is that the best you can say about it? It's downright uncanny, never mind queer! Where in hell is everybody? It's—it's inconceivable that every person can have disappeared," he went on, mystified.

"We've got to look around, Nick. There's Sheila, too! Good Lord, if she's gone as well—"

"We'll look around," Nick interrupted briefly, and strode off towards the spaceship.

IN five minutes they were in the air again, flying slowly at about five hundred feet over New York, passing between the towers of Manhattan, staring down on the streets below. What they saw only served to stagger their minds still further.

Automobiles were piled up in wild and smashed array, buses stood up like islands in the shambles. Traffic in its entirety had gone mad, run into itself and jammed the main streets in the most unholy chaos. Yet nowhere was there a person, nowhere a sign of life. No human walked, no animal slunk along, no bird flew in the heavens.

Westwards to the harbour regions, it was the same. Ships lay either at anchor, rising gently with the tide, else they were piled up in slowly sinking ruin against the jetties. Some were even smashed and interlocked with each other, half settled in shallow waters and black mud.

Blake could not help shivering a little as he stared across the gentle sea towards the horizon. It was utterly empty – no friendly curl of smoke... He looked back over New York. There was not a single wisp of smoke there, either. No factories were in action. The calm was harrowing in its peacefulness. Only the green things lived, as of yore. The trees, the soft grass of the parks, stirring in the cool wind.

"Nick, I can't stand this!" Blake gasped out at last. "It's driving me nuts! I'm only just beginning to realize the horrible fact that there's nobody around anymore! We're alone, man—alone! Do you begin to realize it?"

"Yeah—sure." Nick spoke laconically, but he was manifestly deeply moved. "Just the same there's no reason for going off half-cocked. All things have an explanation—even this!"

"*Everybody's dead...*" Blake muttered.

"Anything but! If that were so, there'd be corpses around. Corpses don't vanish in two weeks, though they smell plenty. No; I don't believe anybody died, though they certainly vanished."

"Surely not everybody in the world...?"

"I dunno..." Nick relapsed into thought for a moment and then shrugged. "I guess it's not worth circumnavigating the globe to try and find out. The radio will do just as well. Keep on flying around while I see what I can pick up."

He settled himself before the apparatus, switched it on. With deliberate persistency, he tried all the leading radio stations of the United States, without a single response. Then, his face becoming graver, he tried London, Paris, Berlin, Moscow, even Sydney and remote other-hemisphere stations... Silence!

Quietly he switched off, stroked his chin moodily.

"Well?" Blake demanded impatiently. "What the devil are you going broody about? What do we *do*?"

"I've no idea—yet. The situation is a most amazing one, Blake. We've got to get used to the incredible fact that we're probably the only two people in the whole world! There may be others, but I'm beginning to doubt it."

"Before I do anything, I'm going to try and find Sheila," Blake said resolutely. "She's got to be around somewhere," he went on desperately. "If she's gone too, I – I don't know what I'll do!"

Nick shrugged. "We can go and see anyway," he commented, in a voice that was anything but optimistic.

Blake's jaw squared purposefully. He drove the ship down towards the main street wherein the girl's apartment block was situated. Gently, he settled near the smashed remains of two interlocked automobiles. With scarce a moment's delay, he had the airlock open and was racing up the steps of the building. The place was quite deserted.

After a brief glance around, he pelted up the stairs to the third floor, savagely rapped on the panels of No. 16—but there was no response. He tried the door: it was securely locked. Nick appeared on the corridor, frowning pensively.

"No answer, I suppose?" he inquired quietly.

Blake nodded bitterly, applied his massive shoulder to the door. "Give me a hand here, will you?"

Under their joint efforts, the lock screws began to give way. They plunged into the apartment at last, cannoned into the table in the centre of the room, and went sprawling.

Blake scrambled to his feet and gazed anxiously around him. The room, save for the overturned table, was just as it had always been, dainty and feminine—but it was dusty everywhere, and the flowers in the window had fallen limply into decaying petals.

With hungry eyes, he strode into the other rooms, calling the girl's name as he went. No response. Nothing appeared to be disturbed. The bed had not been slept in. Scowling, he returned to the lounge and found Nick thoughtfully reading a black leather-bound book.

"This is a swell time to read!" Blake snapped. "Why can't you give me a hand to locate Sheila?"

Nick shrugged. "I picked this up as I straightened the table; must have fallen off when we knocked it over. It's Sheila's diary."

"And what right have you to read it?" Blake glowered at him.

"Oh, have some sense!" Nick retorted impatiently. "I'm not reading the darned thing for the love of it. I thought I might find some sort of a clue, and I'm not so sure that I haven't..." He stopped and grinned faintly. "There are one or two juicy references to you, all the same. You're mentioned as the only guy that matters; rugged, blond manhood and—"

Blake snatched the book in annoyance, gazed at the entries. In silence, he studied the final entry for September 26, the day of the collision. The writing ceased in mid-sentence with a long, whirling stroke of the pen.

"Interesting, eh?" Nick murmured.

Blake grunted, read the entry again thoughtfully.

"I can hardly believe that Blake is so many millions of miles away in space. What a wonderful thing he and Nick are going to see—something I too could have seen if only dad had given me permission. Still, maybe after all I will be able—"

Then the streak of ink and significant emptiness to the bottom of the page. Blake closed the book slowly, puzzling. At last he glanced at Nick.

"Any ideas?"

"Not very clear ones. It's pretty obvious that Sheila was suddenly and unexpectedly interrupted. She left her sentence unfinished—had a shock of some kind too, which accounts for the nervous jolt of the pen. The pen itself isn't around anywhere, which seems rather odd...We don't know when she wrote this. September 26, yes, but at what time? The star collision was not until 8:13 in the evening. Was this written before or after that happening? What happened? Where did everybody go?"

"Fourth dimension!" Blake said abruptly; but Nick shook his head.

"I guess not. A fourth dimension can't be added to, or angled into, the normal three dimensions without some very good reason. Besides, if it were four dimensional, it would incorporate everything—buildings, trees, humans, and probably whole continents. We find everything just as it has always been, with the one exception that all humans, animals, fish and so forth have vanished like mist."

"It's Sheila I'm worrying about," Blake muttered. "She may be in some horrible place, possibly even dead. Good Heavens, suppose there was an invasion from another planet while we were away?" he finished in alarm. "Suppose everybody was carried away?"

Nick signed. "You're the only one that's getting carried away. Talk sense! What possible invasion could there be that takes every living thing, animals and the rest of 'em included, and yet does not even scar a single brick on any building? Besides, all the planets are lifeless, and those in the remoter deeps of space are too far away to bother about... No, it wasn't an invasion. It was some complex slip-up of Nature that we've got to solve. We have all the world's resources at our disposal, the rest of our lives to do it on. Best thing we can do is get back to headquarters and start in to do a little puzzling. Let's go!"

Blake nodded slowly, picked up Sheila's diary reverently, then followed his friend out of the room...

WHILE Nick went into a huddle with himself in the pilots' mess at headquarters, Blake wandered about the deserted metropolis and loaded himself up with tinned foodstuffs from the empty stores. Ordinary food was turning bad, a fact which brought to his mind the possibility of disease.

"We can haul all the fresh food we can find into the open and pour kerosene over it," was Nick's observation, as he sat eating corned beef and drinking coffee in the mess room. "I don't think there's a great deal of danger, anyway. That comes from dead bodies, not putrefied meat. Nevertheless, we'll take precautions."

He turned back to the notes he had made and pondered for a while, chewing rhythmically. Presently he spoke again.

"I think the only way to get to the bottom of this mystery is to make a scientific reconstruction, just as one would a crime. We have one good basis to work from—namely, two stars have never collided in astronomical history within our knowledge, and therefore the effects of such a collision have never been recorded. When it happened before—a near-collision—Earth and the planets were born and later came life. Now here is the question: Is it possible that upon the near or actual collision of two suns, certain types of radiation are emitted that alter the nature of space itself? Life, as we know it, is still a mystery. Maybe it was an accident, or maybe the *potential* for life was produced by a particular radiation that occurred at the crossing of our sun and the runaway. Life did not immediately appear, of course, but the elements of life were present right from the beginning. When the Earth cooled, the chemical reaction of life took place. For millions of years life has gone on..."

"So?" Blake questioned, moodily stirring his coffee.

"Far away in space a similar accident happens again—and life just disappears," Nick said slowly. "The perfect balance, so long undisturbed, was upset."

Blake stared at him. "Are you trying to say that life just—just dissolved, or something?" he demanded.

"Well, life did vanish, didn't it?"

"But where to?" Blake yelled, leaping to his feet. "It's all very well standing around theorizing, but can't we get some action on the matter?"

Nick's dark eyes were gleaming strangely. "Maybe we will," he breathed. "I've got several ideas, and one or another of 'em ought to be right. Something happened when those stars collided; a radiation of some kind infused space and we of all other fleshly things survived because of the proofed walls of our ship. Judging from the hangars, all the spaceships were grounded when the disturbance hit Earth, which explains why only we survive...Yes, I believe I've got something to work on."

He turned suddenly. "I'm going over to the lab to make some experiments," he said briefly. "You do what you like, only don't bother me. I've got to nail this idea whilst it's hot."

Blake nodded slowly. He was haunted by the growing conviction that humanity had gone for all time—that Sheila Berick was only a glorious memory.

CHAPTER III

"THE DISKS"

DAYS passed into weeks and the fall changed to early winter conditions as Nick still struggled day by day to produce some practical line of explanation for the mystery. Several times he read Sheila's diary, but made no comments, always returning it to Blake's sheltering hands. That diary was the only real memory of Sheila he had left.

The rest of the time, Nick spent either in the libraries in the city, or else bringing home electrical machinery on an old truck. The machinery he proceeded to mount in the laboratory, though time and again he pulled it down, sat for days in scowling thought surrounded by books, then started to rebuild again. What he was getting at remained a complete mystery to Blake.

For his part, the inactivity palled on his nerves. He played the role of housekeeper and spent much of his time collecting tinned food from the city stores. The rest of the time he just wandered around, usually took the space machine and toured the empty country, trying vainly to accustom himself to the vision of a world depopulated, flogging his brain to explain it all.

Then there was always that eternal silence, maddening and complete. When time allowed, he travelled with bullet-like velocity to other countries, gazed sombrely down on empty England with its rusting cities, the grass springing up in the streets, the moss sprouting over the corroding hulks of buses and cars. Everywhere there was litter and brown leaves whirling in the winter wind.

The world over it was the same. Rust—decay—death!

Blake found it singularly ironical to tour the world's armament dumps—infinite square miles of war material, added to year by year. Shells were now covered in rust, factories falling into disrepair. Aircraft by the thousands were dusty and neglected. All these mighty preparations for defence or offence—no man had ever really known which—were now lying dead and useless, unwanted, turning back slowly to their primal state. Vast, wasted effort!

Indeed, he found only one thing of interest in his travels. On one tour he visited Mount Wilson observatory, spent the greater part of the evening scanning the heavens through one of the smaller telescopes. The larger ones, motivated by machinery, were out of the question, owing to the world-wide failure of power. He started out with the object of discovering if by any chance space itself could explain the departure of humanity—and ended up with a discovery he had never intended making! Mars had changed!

Without question, the red planet was different. The vast ochre deserts were smothered with curious black marks, extending from pole to pole. What it implied was beyond guessing, but it certainly suggested some kind of life. But why should there be life on a world that had been so long dead? Blake himself knew that the red planet was empty; he had explored it from end to end.

Baffled, Blake finally departed, put his discovery to Nick's analytical brain. Nick was not over-impressed.

"If life can vanish from Earth as it has, it is quite possible that the wave produced effects on Mars, since it would also be included," he said thoughtfully. "Maybe Mars is starting on a new life cycle just as ours faded out."

"Is it worth going to look?" Blake asked keenly.

"Maybe it is, but I've more important things to do. If you'd like to wait until I've finished my experiments, we can go together. It needs two of us in space, you know..."

And at that the matter lay in abeyance for a time.

IN mid-November, the first snowfall of the winter arrived, whirling through feral New York with biting savagery, whisked along by an eighty-mile-an-hour gale. Its roaring moan was the only sound outside the Enterprise Building.

Blake, held up by the weather from further touring, mooched around the mess, taking stuff from the supplies, sitting before the electric stove, in action again now that Nick had fixed the Company's self-generated plant, driven from a specially constructed bore from the Hudson.

Nick himself was over at the laboratory, as usual, across the tarmac square formed by the half-circle of buildings. What he was doing, Blake could only guess at.

Moodily, he got up and went to the window, stared out over the white carpet of the square, the whirling flakes. Then he became alert again as Nick suddenly appeared in the laboratory doorway, his coat tails flying. Nothing but the greatest urgency could have caused Nick to behave so hurriedly. He started to run, his mouth open as though he were shouting.

Blake swung round and ripped open the mess door. In a moment, he had raced along the corridor and down to the lower ground floor. Then, on the steps of the building, he stopped in stunned amazement. Nick was fading oddly as he approached! His breathless, ebbing words were snatched away by the wind.

"I was... the disks..."

Then he vanished! Blake started in stunned horror at a vision of footprints in the snow leading half across the huge square, then abruptly ceasing.

"Nick!" he screamed suddenly. "Nick! Where are you?"

Only the savage wind answered, and the snow, piling thick and gentle against the walls, melting in the warmer air of the big doorway. Heedless, Blake dashed outside and plunged around like a madman, staring at the baffling footprints, gazing dazedly into emptiness.

Hardly aware of what he was doing, he finally blundered into the laboratory, closed the door, and stood breathing heavily with his back against it. With a vast effort, he fought for control over himself, tried to still his hammering heart.

At last he sank down weakly on a solitary chair amidst a mass of strange, puzzling machinery, looked dully around him on generators, tubes and coils, insulator banks and switchboards. Predominant among the whole gamut of stuff was a horseshoe-shaped magnet. None of the machinery was at work now, though there was a certain heated air about the place, a smell like hot oil that seemed to indicate it had not long been idle.

Blake was calmer now. He tried to face with courage the staggering realization that he was one man alone in all the world, surrounded by scientific mysteries. What were the fading words Nick had uttered? Something about "Disks..."

He turned and began to look about him, but all his searching failed to reveal anything that might pass as a disk. At last, he gave it up and went over the rest of the machinery instead. He began to see why Nick had gone to such effort in the past weeks to collect all this stuff, though its purpose was still as obscure as ever.

Blake cursed his lack of engineering knowledge, his relatively sparse conceptions of science. Space-piloting was his profession, and because he had made it his speciality, other pursuits had gone to the wall. Now he regretted the fact.

Gingerly, he tried the switches on the board, and after a while succeeded in getting the generators going—driven of course by the sunken Hudson bore turbine plant—then just as quickly switched them off for fear of trouble. He would have to make a complete study of the whole business, before daring to do anything rash. Otherwise he might blow himself sky high.

Not that it mattered, he reflected bitterly. He was alone now and—of course, there was that mysterious life on Mars. Life of another planet? Not his own kind? Blake shook his head moodily; there was little advantage in exploring its possibilities.

HE spent another hour studying Nick's notes, but they were in the advanced jargon of the professional scientist and made little sense to him. He could hardly understand the symbols, much less piece together their meaning. In the end, he returned wearily across the square to the mess room, sat down and relapsed into thought. Time and again that last incredible vision of Nick disappearing into thin air kept returning to him.

What had the laboratory machines had to do with it? Why had he so suddenly disappeared? Blake rubbed his unshaven chin in perplexity, drummed on his out-thrust legs in bafflement. Back of his mind was dim hope that Nick would return. But the hours passed by and nothing happened.

The ghastly, maddening silence continued, rendered doubly intense by the softly falling, blanketing snow. At last the night closed down, wild and bitter, with the wind howling with increased fury around the great building, snow piling thick on the window ledges, whirling across the darkened square.

Blake still sat on before the electric stove, food and drink forgotten.

"Only man in the world..." he kept muttering to himself. "Only man in the world..."

He thought of the immensities of outer space as he knew them—the eternal reaches of the infinite, the coldly winking stars, always friendless, always cruel. He thought of the great barren world around him, the endless miles of decaying ruins, the shipless seas. Only the plants still lived, and they too were asleep now that winter had come. No living thing to talk to—all of the joys of human companionship, the eternal struggle for existence, the hopes, the fears, the achievements—wiped out!

"It's more than any man can stand!" he shouted hoarsely, at last, leaping to his feet—and with sudden fury, he kicked his stool across the room. It struck his own particular metal locker with considerable violence, clicked the door open. With savage strides, he went across to close it, then stopped as his eyes fell to the little black book on the top shelf.

Sheila's diary. His passion drained from him. Gently, he took the book out, fingered it, gazed at it with hungry eyes. Slowly he turned the gold-edged pages, read words he had never been intended to read, the bare revelations of Sheila's heart. He realized for the first time how deeply she had really loved him.

He forgot his loneliness for a while in reading the clear words, but it all filled him with a brooding sense of helplessness as he realized they were but the shadow memories of a girl he would never meet again, the recordings of one woman in millions who had gone into an Unknown. Then as he neared the end of the notes, he paused, frowned at what was clearly a recent coffee stain on the delicate paper. Sheila? Would she have been so careless with her revered diary? It was out of the question that she had ever allowed anybody else to read her notes, unless...

"Nick!" Blake breathed suddenly. "So he read all through this diary when he kept borrowing it—" he broke off, frowning at the page. Apart from the stain, it was dirty and thumb-marked, had plainly been read many times. He studied it closely, trying to find meaning in the words that had obviously interested Nick so deeply. The entry was for September 24, two days before the final entry.

"To kill time tonight I went to hear Professor Cardell's lecture on the limitations of life. But either it was not very interesting, or else I'm very dull. He tried to prove by mathematics how thin is the hairline between creation and extinction of fleshly life, so thin indeed that the merest variation of cosmic forces might pitch the balance in the wrong direction. I think I'm fairly intelligent, but I couldn't follow him... I wonder how far away dear Blake is now?"

"Variation of cosmic forces?" Blake muttered, frowning. "I

wonder if—No, it's impossible."

But even as he repudiated his notions, something knocked hard in his reasoning. Nick had been no fool, and he'd seen something in that observation to demand a considerable study of it. Professor Cardell? Blake remembered the name vaguely...

He examined the diary again, but no page had received such attention as that particular one. He read the final tragic entry again, then he put the book carefully in his pocket and ate a belated meal. But his thoughts were busy again now, dashing the deep melancholia from his mind.

At last, he reached a decision.

He went over to the laboratory again and, carrying a portable lamp around with him, finally unearthed a pile of books he had noticed on earlier visits. They were what he had hoped for—a whole series of books by Cardell brought by Nick from the public libraries.

Triumphantly he put them down on the bench and began to study them, aided in places by the blue pencilled portions Nick had evidently considered of particular value. He read on and on—far into the night.

CHAPTER IV

RECIPE FOR SUICIDE!

BLAKE found it hard going! His none too scientific mind grappled with the high-flown phrasing and technique. He had no early work up, but plunged straight away into the advanced enigma of science.

He made his quarters in the laboratory, and sat there hour after hour, day after day, except for the intervals for meals. He pored over Cardell's books, but the theories of life expounded therein were so complex, he made but little progress...

After a week of pondering, he was but little nearer the truth than he had been at first. In that week, he had been subconsciously aware of almost continuous snowstorms, aided no doubt by the absolute lack of warmth from buildings and chimneys ascending into the air. He found he was pretty well snowbound in the laboratory.

He slept there, had his meals there, gazed out on the carpet of white, pondered whether he should make an effort to reach Mars; then thinking better of it, he looked around at the machines.

"Somehow, these have got to be solved," he muttered. "There may even be the chance that Nick was swivelled into another section of space. If he went, others might have gone before him. Sheila might even be there... Wonder what he meant by disks?"

He rubbed his head in bewilderment, stared absently at the abandoned radio, then suddenly he noticed something he had never seen before. The radio was switched over to the recording control... Instantly his eye followed the length of cabling from the radio apparatus to a self-recording machine in the corner.

"Of course!" he muttered. "Am I an idiot! Disks! Records! Self-made records... now, let me see..."

He dived for the big cabinet under the recording machine and flung the doors wide. His eyes gleamed at the sight of a dozen small disks nearly numbered and fully indented with sound track.

"So that was what he meant." Blake breathed. "He recorded his impressions. Just like Nick: methodical to the last. Why didn't he say recordings in the first place?"

He put on the first disk, switched on to playback, and stood waiting expectantly. Nick's recorded voice spoke.

"This is the voice of Nick Vane. Probably it will be you, Blake, who'll hear me. In any case, anybody understanding English will know what I'm talking about. I've recorded matters like this because it is much easier to give my findings by talking than by writing them down – much faster, too. Another reason is, I'm not at all sure how my experiments are going to work out, and on the off chance that something may happen to me suddenly, I'm leaving a sure-fire explanation behind me. If I should happen to suddenly vanish, you will know that the theory I'm going to outline is the true one.

"Some time ago I mooted over the idea that the collision of those two stars in space had done something queer to earthly life. At that time it was a shot in the dark: since then I have backed the theory up with postulations from the works of Cardell, who knew more about earthly life any man alive. Earthly life exists only in very rigid limits. It came into being in the first place by a radiation from space—induced when our sun and a runaway crossed each other—and happened to be of just the right combination of wavelengths to produce life.

"Cardell has only enlarged a trifle on the original theories of Sir James Jeans when he wrote his *Mysterious Universe*. Jeans said —and quite truly as I have since proven— 'It becomes increasingly likely that what specially distinguishes the matter of living bodies is the quite commonplace element carbon, always in conjunction with other atoms with which it forms exceptionally large molecules. If that be so, life only exists in the universe because the carbon atom possesses such exceptional properties. Again, the carbon atom consists of six electrons revolving around the central nucleus, thereby differing from its two nearest neighbours in the table of chemical elements—boron and nitrogen—in having one electron more than the, former and one electron fewer than the latter. Yet this slight difference must account in the last analysis for all the difference between life and the absence of life...' That ends Jeans' observations...

"And it's quite true; I've worked it out for myself. Life came into being because the original unique radiation at the birth of the Earth did things to carbon. Since that time, life has steadily progressed with not a thing in the world to disturb it, always hanging on the vague edge of disaster if the balance of the cosmos ever shifted in the least,.

"That shift came! When those two stars collided way out in space, they created a radiation identical with the one that started life on Earth, but this time—because this radiation tried to create life again—it only succeeded in over-stimulating a life already well progressed. Over-stimulation killed it off entirely, just the same as in some experiments, a plant will grow rapidly under a fixed flow of radiation, but will die if it gets an excess. That's what happened. The carbon atom structure just fell to pieces: all fleshly life ceased to be, vanished like mist and the Earth was empty, leaving only the non-carbon forms of life, or at least those which do not entirely rely on it for their basis..."

The disk came to a finish. Blake put on the next one and listened again with a certain growing horror at the cold inevitability of Nick's conclusions.

"I was more than ever sure of the truth of this theory when you, Blake, reported life on Mars. Mars has always been sterile, but it has the same basic possibilities of life as Earth. Its atmosphere, though extremely thin, is suitable. It has a great amount of chemical resources, as we well know. Life could just as easily come to Mars at the moment Earth's finished. On Earth only the carbon-assimilating forms of life survived—such as trees and vegetation, but the direct carbon creations vanished.

"I have to admit one thing: I owe a lot to Sheila Berick's diary. If it hadn't been for her going to Cardell's lecture that night, I'd have wandered around plenty before finding the right clue.

"There was only one way to prove the possibility of my theory to the uttermost, and that was by trying it out! Hence this recording in case I'm successful. You'll appreciate that it is a better way to give it than by odd snatches and drifts of personal conversation. In this way, you have all the facts before you. Funny thing, but I notice in my recording I speak as though events have already happened. Wonder if it's premonition?

"When I wanted to try out the theory for myself, I realized that I was faced with certain difficulties. The etheric wave generated by the celestial collision could not happen again in history without the almost impossible occurrence of another collision. No use waiting for that. I considered the exact happenings at a celestial collision— the tremendous gravitational and stress fields set up, the spreading of the radiation's influence. Most of the clues I got from our recording apparatus aboard the ship, which definitely gave all de-tails and showed conclusively how we had been saved by our ship's repulsion shield. How could I reproduce the collision of two suns in a laboratory?"

Again Blake changed the records.

"That had me floored for the time being, then I arrived at so simple a solution, I was quite amazed at myself. The collision of two suns is fundamentally the same thing as collision of electron and proton. One belongs to the macrocosm and the other to the microcosm, but the effects are identical in that they produce, the self-same radiation, the only difference being the enormously lesser scale of distance in the case of the microcosm.

"I suppose that I produced atomic force when I annihilated the protons and electrons of a piece of potassium forcing the released energy through special transformers. The influence radiated by the horseshoe magnet was very brief and limited. It satisfied me though, so much so I set to work to make these recordings because I'm going to try the thing again.

"If anything should happen to me, you'll find instructions in disks eight and nine about how to control the thing. I'm going to set about that recording now—"

Blake took off the finished disk thoughtfully and stroked his chin

"So he was right in his ideas," he muttered. "Only thing I can think of is that when he made the final test, he got scared and made a dash for it. The influence of the magnet caught up with him and disintegrated him utterly. I was just out of reach and escaped... Hell! What a ghastly thought to chew over!"

He looked moodily around at the apparatus, at the snow-covered windows.

"Now that I know the truth, I'm not much better off," he grunted. "Everybody's dead, Sheila included. I'm just the last man on the Earth with one card left up my sleeve... I can commit suicide more elaborately than most guys..."

He swung around with sudden savage determination, snatched out disks eight and nine, put number eight on the machine, and listened carefully, scribbling down the detailed instructions Nick gave on the working of the machinery and switch manipulation.

It took him an hour to get it all down, then he switched the recording apparatus off and pondered his notes. His whole being now was mastered by an intense anxiety to get the thing done—get away from this eternal silence and drifting snow. At last he got to his feet, walked slowly around the machinery as he studied the directions, identified each separate piece of mechanism and attendant switches, opened the floor trapdoor and listened critically to the thunderous roaring of the deeply-sunken Hudson bore, the waters swollen by melting snow.

So far as he could tell, everything was in order. He searched for the necessary piece of potassium on the chemical side of the laboratory, placed it in the disintegrating chamber. Then; very cautiously, he closed the required switches one by one and listened to the dynamos taking up the whine of power.

His further movements were less confident. He had the vague feeling at the back of his mind that he ought to give the directions closer study—but against that he had weighed the necessity for immediate action and the desire to get out of this deserted world as quickly as possible.

CHAPTER V

TRACKS IN THE SNOW!

HE worked on doggedly until well into the winter afternoon, adjusting the apparatus, the directions firmly held in his hand—and the more he progressed, the more his admiration for Nick's genius increased.

He had devised an apparatus of amazing ingenuity and automatic surety to produce the desired effects. Even to him, it must have been difficult. To Blake it was meaningless. His actions were simply directed towards a given end. Of the intricacies, he knew less than nothing.

He stopped only once for a meal, then resumed as the winter darkness closed down. At last he had come to the final switch, the throwing of which would set the automatic apparatus into action by bringing in the dynamos. Within fifteen seconds, according to Nick, the atoms of the potassium in the disintegrating chamber would be crushed by nameless forces, their energy driven through specially constructed machinery and transformers to the outlet magnet.

Blake looked around pensively and stroked his bristly chin.

"Hope it works," he muttered. "Not that it matters much anyway."

For a fraction of a second he hesitated, then closed the master switch. At the sudden roar of power from the released machines, he backed to the door, opened it wide, and stood with his back to the piled-up snow outside. The icy wind whistled around him, ruffling his unkempt hair, chilling him after the warmth of the laboratory.

He felt very much like a man with a lighted bomb in his hands. Before him was the savagely working mechanism –behind him, the night and the snow. The electric light reflected back from the polished machines in their brazen, invincible array. For some reason, in those moments, he wondered if he wanted to die after all. Odd! He could think of hundreds of things he could do if he went on living. Suppose he didn't die, was horribly mangled instead!

His eyes fixed on the great magnet...Then something happened!

One of the machines near the wall started to glow red hot, sent little whirls of blue smoke into the air from burning armatures. The stench of burning rubber arose instantly.

In an instant, Blake realized what had happened. Somewhere he had made a wrong connection, perhaps positive to negative leads, and the thing was short-circuiting. He looked desperately around, and at that identical instant, the red-hot machine came to an abrupt standstill, automatically cut out the other machines. The wall behind the faulty machine began to scorch dangerously—a sheet of flame leaped suddenly from smouldering rubber and shot towards the chemicals on the shelf above.

Blake staggered back before a rush of superheated air. An explosion dinned in his ears. He went reeling into soft snow and lay half-buried in it as splintering glass and pieces of metal flew over his head with devastating force. Then, at last, he dared to raise himself gently out of the white wetness, turned slowly and gazed helplessly at leaping, soaring flames from the laboratory. Within seconds, the whole place had become an inferno, well prepared by the inflammable chemicals and materials within it. Before his very eyes, everything was being destroyed—even the disks containing the instructions.

That brought him to his feet and he ploughed through the snow towards the open doorway, only to stagger back helplessly before the terrific heat. No use trying to save anything. March into the flames? He shook his head... Not that way!

He stood with bitter eyes, his fists clenched, watching the flames crackling to the snow-ridden sky. The fire would no doubt confine itself to the laboratory and not affect the rest of the great building. Did that matter?

"What does anything matter any more?" Blake asked himself slowly. "I didn't commit suicide that way, but there are other ways."

Inwardly, he knew he had only himself to blame for the failure of the machinery. He had hurried over the matter—should have read the notes more carefully.

Furiously he swung around, hands deep in trouser pockets, and regardless of the bitter wind and whirling flakes, he plunged through the knee-high snow away from the blaze—to anywhere, so long as he could try to collect his thoughts and stop himself from going mad. He realized that he was dangerously close to it, and to brood indoors, in the pilots' mess perhaps, was no way to cure himself. Better be lost in this mad, white world... Much better. The idea grew to an obsession.

HE had no idea which way he went, whither he intended going.

It was the same in all directions, anyhow. Pitch darkness, whirling snow, icy wind. His hands were already numb from exposure, his legs soaked to the knees.

Now and again he raised his face to the screaming dark, realized subconsciously that he was following one of the former suburban roads to the centre of New York...

Might be a good idea to keep on walking until he dropped. Death from cold. He had heard it wasn't so bad, at that. Sleepiness... extinction. Why not?

"Go on, blow!" he snarled to the wind. "Who the hell cares, anyway?"

He went on stubbornly, determined to walk until he could walk no longer. Time and again he fell into deep drifts, stumbled over objects covered in snow, found rusting automobiles buried nearly to their tops.

In the midst of the whirling darkness of New York, the snow was waist deep, reflecting back to him in the odd way snow has in the midst of the darkest night.

The metropolis was a city of ghostliness, its tall spires still rearing invincibly to the heavens. The snowflakes seemed wetter here; somewhere behind the ragged clouds a moon was trying to struggle through.

"Why should all this have to happen to one man?" Blake demanded, stumbling along. "Why should I, of all the people that were once on the Earth, be doomed to die alone?—more alone than any man has ever been since the world began?"

The moan of the wind was the only answer.

He went on more slowly, stared at the long white-ridden vista ahead of him, with the buildings rising darkly on either side of it. How different it all was, how different from the New York, of old times!

He smiled twistedly. He was beginning to feel sleepy at last. He hardly knew he had a body; it was frozen through and through.

The moon came briefly from between flying clouds, turned the world around him to sepulchral, gleaming white.

His smile broadened to a laugh—then the laugh faded from his lips as that transient moonlight revealed something to him—marks through the snow!—Marks such as a body might make—such as his own body had made behind him.

The trail stretched right ahead of him.

"No!" he whispered, shaking his snow-covered head. "No, I'm dreaming it! I'm falling asleep!"

But he knew that was not true.

He forced himself onwards again by main strength. The moon vanished once more, but he could see enough by reflection. There was the trail of somebody or something, quite recently made, and it came from somewhere on the right, had now joined his own trail. If it had been a human, the person had been waist deep in snow; if an animal, it could only have been a giant dog or a horse, a possibility that seemed highly unlikely.

Mad pulsating joy suddenly raced through Blake. Something else was alive in this sepulchre of a world!

"Ahoy!" he yelled desperately. "Ahoy! Where are you?"

There was no sign of a response, and his wild hopes sank a little. Probably there'd be a very ordinary explanation at the end of the trail. His numbness was a nuisance now, and so was this raging desire to go to sleep. The very thing he'd set out to do looked likely to prove his undoing.

"Why should it be?" he roared out furiously, thrashing himself into activity. "Why should everything sour on me? This is one rap I'm not taking—"

The activity he suddenly conjured up was terrific—and it did him good. It helped to restore his sluggish circulation, rid him of his numbness. The going was easier now, too; the unknown one had ploughed a trail for him and the moon was coming out in increasingly long spells.

HE found at last that he had reached the centre of the street. What street it was, he had not troubled to notice. His whole attention was concentrated on the fact that the trail had suddenly turned off to a large open doorway. He followed it avidly and the snow thinned off, was ankle deep—then only sole-thick. With blank amazement, he looked down at the granite step of the building. There was the distinct imprint of shoes, hardly even blurred by more recent snow—

A woman's shoes!

"Now I know I'm crazy!" Blake looked around him with burning eyes. Then he abruptly realized where he was—Sheila Berick's apartment building!

Instantly he took a step back into the snow and stared up at the rearing facade to where he knew her window was situated. At the higher levels, the snow had not encased the windows so thickly, blown away by the wind. Blake wondered if his heart stopped beating when in the window on the third floor he detected a faint evidence of light, such as a candle might make.

"Sheila?" he breathed through dry lips. "Can it...?" His heart started to pound again. He swung around, plunged through the open doorway like a lunatic and charged for the stairs.

"Sheila!" he screamed frantically. "Sheila! Sheila!" and the great building rang with the echoes of his cry.

Up he went, slipping in the darkness, slamming into the walls and hardly feeling it. He arrived at last on the third floor corridor, stopped dead. There was yellow light shining from the open doorway of the girl's room. He remembered he and Nick had smashed the lock.

"Sheila!" he called gently.

Still no answer. Hardly daring to imagine what he might find, he tip-toed forward, peered around the door jamb. The room was pretty much as he and Nick had left it, save that a candle, burned low, stood on the table now. Its pale, flickering glow cast upon a motionless, heavily coated figure sprawled face down on the carpet.

Instantly Blake reached down, turned the figure over and gazed stupidly into the white face and closed eyes, the dark hair peeping under the fur hat... It was Sheila!

He muttered things he hardly understood—then with a sudden effort he raised her, carried her into the next room and laid her on the bed. He returned for the candle, then forcing himself to calmness, he set to work. The first horrible thought that the girl was dead was banished as he detected the slow beat of her pulse. Immediately, he searched around and found brandy, soaked his handkerchief in water, and bathed her forehead.

IT seemed hours to him before she finally stirred, opened her eyes wearily. Gradually they became puzzled, regarded his face in bafflement.

"Blake!" she whispered. "How—how did you—?"

"Sheila," he murmured gently, seizing her in his arms. "How did you ever come to escape the dissolution of life? *How*?"

"Dissolution of life?" she repeated, surprise dashing all the haziness out of her mind. "What dissolution?"

Blake stared at her. "But—but like everybody else, you were surely caught up in the radiation that destroyed all life?" he cried. "I'd given you up for dead!"

"The girl rose to a sitting position, her eyes amazed in the light of the candle.

"Just what are you talking about?" she demanded.

Solemnly he told her the details. When he finished, she shuddered.

"So that is why the whole world seemed so empty and deserted when I landed late this afternoon!" she murmured. "I saw out in space how deserted it all looked. I was frightened—Oh, of course, you don't understand even now. It really isn't so mysterious. You know I wanted to go with you on that trip into space?"

"Uh-huh," Blake acknowledged.

"Well, father was against that, of course—but I decided I might try and join you on your return trip. I wanted to see that collision from space where I could have an uninterrupted view. I bribed one of the pilots to take me. He said it would be difficult, but if he could work it, he'd telephone me. He managed it all right, but we were desperately short of time. I had to dash away on the instant..."

"Then that's why you left your diary on the table?"

Sheila nodded rather shyly. "Yes; I was writing it when Hawkins—the pilot—rang up. I was so pent up with excitement, the sudden ring of the bell made me jump like a fool. That explains the streak at the end of my writing."

"Then what happened?" Blake persisted.

"Well, we were well out in the inner circle of space—that is, on this side of the outer planets—when the collision of the stars happened. We saw it beautifully, but a moment afterwards the ship rocked violently. Hawkins and I were thrown over. I was stunned by banging my head on a fixed chair, but poor Hawkins, I found later, had broken his neck. I found we were drifting in space, our nearest field of attraction being Mars. I don't know much about space ships, but I did know enough standard emergency procedure to manage to activate the ship's automatic pilot, which braked the ship's fall and made a landing on the red planet.

"To my amazement, I found the planet teeming with rudimentary, fast evolving life, passing through all the stages that Earth-life has had since the earliest times. Vegetation, adapted to the thin air, is springing up. It can only mean that life has come to Mars in just the same way that it was banished from Earth, but for some reason—maybe because of the lesser gravity and lighter air— it is evolving at terrific speed. Eventually, I imagine, Mars will have life of a class and intellect close to our own!

"I stayed there until I had recovered my strength, then I started back for Earth. The automatic pilot made the journey possible. This evening I touched. Earth, had seen beforehand the deserted state of everything. The snow was tremendously thick when I left the ship. I got to my room here, was baffled to find the door lock smashed. I was afraid—of the silence. I found a candle and lighted it, then I think that the cold air after the long confinement in the space ship, my weariness and fright, suddenly reacted on me. I remember nothing more until I found you bending over me."

Blake smiled. "So simple! I know there is a new life on Mars; I saw it myself through the telescope. If only I had counted the number of ships in the space-hangar I'd have found one short, but the idea never occurred to me. Hawkins took a risk, I guess. But that's beside the point. Thank God you decided to do what you did —otherwise we would have been separated forever. So these Martians are evolving fast, are they?"

Sheila nodded slowly. "Very fast."

Blake smiled a little. "We have an entire world here, only waiting to be tenanted. We have the knowledge, and the science—"

He broke off and gripped the girl's arm. "Why not?" he breathed. "If we can scrape along somehow for the next few years, we can then start putting ideas forward to the Martians. We're going to destroy all the great armament dumps located in various parts of the world. We'll start out fair and square."

"I'm with you," Sheila smiled.

"It won't be so long," Blake murmured.

They sat looking eagerly at each other in the sputtering light of the candle. The kiss they finally gave each other sounded amazingly noisy in the vast, aching silence of a world waiting to be born anew.